Murder Takes a Bow

An Olivia Morgan Cruise Ship Mystery
Wendy Neugent

SWH Media, LLC

For my grandma, Violet Rose.

Thank you for passing down your love of reading to me and for all of the grocery bags filled with mystery books that you shared with me over the years.

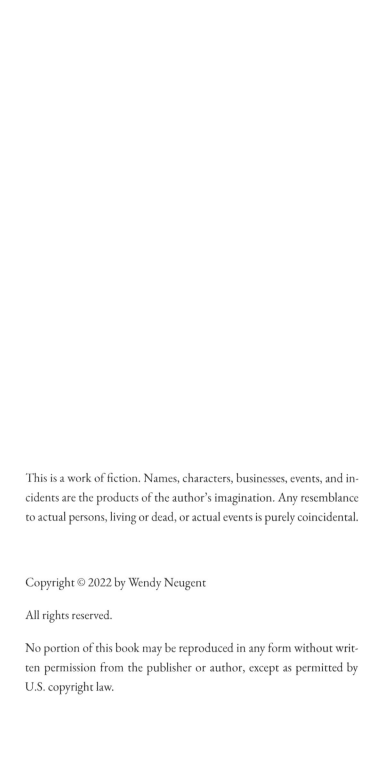

This is a work of fiction. Names, characters, businesses, events, and incidents are the products of the author's imagination. Any resemblance to actual persons, living or dead, or actual events is purely coincidental.

1

O livia glanced at the line of onboarding passengers at the elevators and sighed.

She only had ten minutes to get to her cabin, drop
her bags, and get up to the lifeboat drill.

A passenger walked in front of her and grazed her
foot with his suitcase. Another passenger bumped
into her while looking up at the dramatically lit ceiling
five decks above. The atrium's smoky mirrored walls,
marble-tiled floor, and dramatic art were eye-catching.

She should have used the crew gangway instead of
venturing into the chaotic lobby.

Lounges and shops lined the side of the atrium. A
wide, sweeping stairway circled the bank of elevators,
and tired travelers filled the seating area.

A long line of passengers waited for help with their
accounts or room keys at the purser's desk.

One mother sat next to her three kids. They were
bouncing on the couch like a trampoline. The mother

asked them to stop. She looked defeated, but too tired to do anything about it, when they didn't.

A tuxedoed man sat at a grand piano in the middle of the atrium playing jazz. The heavy sweet scent from the huge flower arrangement on the piano wafted over Olivia as she walked by.

Couples and families waited to get their pictures taken in front of a painted backdrop with a cartoon version of the ship. The ship's photographer, Martin hurriedly posed each group, handing them an orange life ring with 'S. S. Starlight' written on it.

"Cheese!" the passengers shouted in unison as his flash went off.

The photographer took the life ring back and rushed them away from the backdrop. He glanced at the long line waiting for their picture to be taken, as he directed the next group to take their place.

Joseph, a cabin steward, pushed his overloaded brass luggage cart through the crowded lobby.

Olivia backed out of his way and smiled at him as he passed by. He gave her an exhausted half-smile. The stewards had been working all night, picking up luggage from the last group of passengers and getting it ready to be taken off the ship as soon as they had docked. They reversed the process in the afternoon as the passengers embarked. In between they had to get the cabins ready for the new arrivals.

A passenger cut in front of Joseph.

Joseph stopped abruptly to avoid running into him. The luggage on the cart swayed.

Joseph reached up and tried to stop the luggage from collapsing, but he couldn't stop the precariously balanced suitcases from falling off the cart.

One hit the leg of the photographer's tripod, knocking the camera. Joseph grabbed the tripod before the camera fell.

Martin charged toward Joseph. He stood in front of Joseph's face, speaking in a low, threatening voice. "What is wrong with you, you idiot?"

Martin grabbed the tripod out of Joseph's grasp.

"I'm terribly sorry, sir. It was an accident."

"Sorry isn't good enough. You could have broken my extremely expensive camera." Martin poked Joseph in the chest with his finger. "I'm going to report you to your supervisor."

Joseph picked up a fallen suitcase and stacked it back up on the luggage cart.

"Look at me when I am talking to you."

"Yes, sir." Joseph sighed as he stopped and turned toward the photographer.

"Pick up the suitcases and do not walk near my equipment again." Martin glared at Joseph.

Olivia walked towards them and grabbed a purple suitcase off the floor and handed it to Joseph. "Here, let me help you pick up the luggage."

"Oh no, ma'am! I will get it. This is not your job."

"I don't mind. Life is better when we help each other." Olivia looked pointedly at Martin.

Martin began to say something, but Olivia gave him a look that dared him to try. He grunted and turned away towards the next group of passengers waiting to get their picture taken.

Olivia waited while Joseph picked up the last piece of luggage, threw it on top of the luggage cart, and began making his way through the crowd.

Olivia pushed open a heavy crew door that blended into the wall and ducked down a narrow passage. Crew members were racing up and down the hall. They all knew where they were going and walked with purpose instead of milling about like the new passengers. The utilitarian gray metal walls of the narrow passageway stood in stark contrast to the luxurious atrium.

Olivia ran down the crew stairs, her footsteps echoing off the metal walls. She popped out into the passageway right next to her cabin door. She put down her bags, got her key card out of her wallet, and slid it into the lock. The lights flashed green as the lock clicked open. She pushed on the handle to open her cabin door. Holding it open with her foot, she picked up her bags and dragged them in.

Her door shut behind her with a thunk.

She threw the bags on her bed.

"Hey, Baby! How was your day?"

"Hey, Baby!"

"I missed my guy. I bought you some snacks," said Olivia.

"Mmmm, snacks!"

"I got almost everything on my list. I should be able to get the rest in Nassau. What did you do today?"

Chico turned away and peered out the porthole, whistling quietly to himself.

"Ok, then. If you are going to ignore me, I won't give you this."

"Treat?"

"Yeah, I thought that would get your attention. Here you go."

"I love you!"

"I love you, too. Give me a kiss."

Chico shook his wings and strained towards Olivia.

Olivia reached down. "Step up."

Chico lifted his foot towards her. She picked him up off his perch.

"That's my boy,"

Chico made kissing sounds as she pet his green and yellow neck feathers.

"Let's change your water. I bought newspapers to change your cage, too."

Olivia unpacked her shopping bags. She'd been able to get Chico's favorite pellets and treats at the pet store. She pulled the two matching notebooks Peter had asked for out of her shopping bag.

"I hope these are right, Chico. Peter didn't tell me if I should get black or blue notebooks."

Olivia took the notebooks to the desk.

She noticed an envelope with her name on it sitting on the desk.

Her cabin steward usually slipped her mail under the door. He rarely brought it into the cabin.

She picked up the envelope and tore it open.

Olivia sunk down into the desk chair as she read the letter, gasping as the air left her lungs.

Chico squawked.

"Oh buddy, we are in big trouble."

A deep British voice came on over the intercom. "Welcome aboard the Starlight of the Seas. I'm Tristan Waterson and I am your cruise director. We are so glad that you have chosen to cruise with Axis Cruise Line. I look forward to meeting you all at the Bon voyage party, but before we can leave port, every passenger needs to attend our lifeboat drill. Please bring a life jacket for every person in your party. Make your way to the Lido deck, deck 11, now.

Olivia jumped as the ship's horn blasted.

She sat in stunned silence.

A knock at her door brought her back to reality. She opened the door, half expecting it to be Peter, laughing at his joke. Instead, Hayley, her best friend and the singer from the revue show stood in the doorway.

"Hey, you ready to go up to the lifeboat drill? We're going to be late to our muster station."

On autopilot, Olivia grabbed her life jacket and followed Hayley up the stairs.

She mouthed the lifeboat drill steps along with the cruise staff member giving the speech.

Olivia knew what to do in case of an emergency on the cruise ship.

She did not know what to do with the current emergency in her life.

When the lifeboat drill was over, Olivia followed Hayley to the Calypso bar for their traditional post-lifeboat drill cocktail.

They had their choice of seats in the lounge. Most of the passengers were at the Bon Voyage celebration. The bartender swiped their ID cards and they carried their frosty pink cocktails over to their regular table by the window. They liked to watch the ship leave port. Hayley spun her chair to face the window, waiting for the ship to pull away from the dock.

Olivia looked down at her frozen cocktail. Reality came crashing down on her.

Peter was gone.

After ten years of him telling her they'd get married and have a normal life after they got off ships, he'd left her.

Just like that.

She was alone. She was stuck on the ship with their show scheduled in a few days.

No magician, just her, the magic assistant.

Her tears welled up and overflowed down her cheek.

She put down her drink and pushed it away.

Hayley turned back towards Olivia.

"Can you believe we get paid to do this? Whoa, are you crying? What's going on? Are you ok?" asked Hayley.

"I'm absolutely not ok. Peter's gone."

"Gone? He missed the ship?"

"No, like gone, gone. He left me."

"What? You can't be serious,"

"Seriously." Olivia shook her head. "He's gone."

Olivia handed Hayley the letter.

Hayley read the terse note. She paused, looked at Olivia, and then read it again. "That sucker. What the heck?"

"He didn't even give me a reason. He just blew our life up."

"He didn't even have the backbone to tell you in person? I can't believe he did this. Actually, you know what? I can believe it." Hayley pounded the table with her fist. "What a worthless scum bucket. I always thought there was something not quite right about him. You are better off without him."

"I'm not better off! I love him."

"I know you do. I'm sorry I said that. I'm just so angry with him for hurting you." Hayley rubbed Olivia's back.

"My entire life is wrapped up in his. We've lived together, worked together, we've done everything together. I don't know what I am going to do without him."

"You will be ok. I promise"

"On top of everything, he left me on the ship. We have months left on our contract. I can't stay on the ship. But I can't sign off until I get the paperwork done to get the illusions off the manifest so I can ship them home. And I have to get the vet scheduled to sign Chico off."

Olivia's voice quavered, and tears welled up again.

"Oh! I don't even have a home to ship them to! Tristan is going to be livid that he doesn't have a magic act. He's going to kick me off the ship when he finds out Peter is gone. What am I going to do about Chico?

Oh, Hayley. I don't know what to do. This is a disaster."

Hayley picked her Bahama Mama up and took a sip. "Well, I guess we need to make sure Tristan doesn't find out."

"What do you mean? Of course, Tristan needs to know. He needs to call the entertainment director and get a different act flown out to replace us." Olivia's hand shook as she reached for her drink.

She took a big sip of the frozen drink and grimaced. She grabbed her aching forehead."Ah! Brain freeze!"

"Put your tongue on the roof of your mouth. It'll fix the brain freeze. What I meant is that Tristan doesn't need to find out because he has a magic act."

"Hayley, did they already replace us? Did Peter tell them he was leaving, and they brought on another act?"

"No, silly, what I mean is that you are the magic act. You don't need Peter. You are the one who does most of the magic while he just stands there waving his arms around like he's doing something amazing. I've watched you doing all the hard stuff."

"Peter does the hard stuff. He's the one that talks to the audiencc. I could never do the talking part."

"I've watched you perform your show. You are running your tail off, keeping the show going, jumping in and out of boxes, twisting yourself like a pretzel, changing costumes. What does Peter do? Tells some jokes and tries to look mysterious while you are doing all the heavy lifting. Personally, I have always thought it was ridiculous that he got top billing when you were doing everything, and looking beautiful while doing it, I might add."

"I can't do it alone no matter what, so it doesn't really matter what I did before. It's not like I can put flaming spears through myself while I'm in the box."

"No, you're right, you can't do it by yourself. But, we can!"

"What are you talking about?"

"What I'm talking about is that I can wave my arms better than Peter did. Plus, I'm way prettier than him. I'll be your lovely assistant."

Olivia tried to wrap her head around Hayley's proposal.

The intense rumble of the ship's engines startled her.

The anchor clunked as it was raised up.

The ship inched away from the dock.

Hayley shrugged. "You're not getting off the ship. We're leaving port. You can't leave without Chico. So, what other option do you have?"

Olivia closed her eyes and tried to go through the list of illusions they had. Could she and Hayley put enough of them together to do an actual show? What other choice did she have?

Hayley reached across the table and took Olivia's hand in hers. "I'll help you. We'll do it together. It'll be fun, I promise."

"Fun? Not sure how it will be fun, but I'm also not sure what other choice I have."

"It will be fun. You always have fun with me, right?"

Olivia laughed, some of the tension leaving her shoulders. Hayley was right. "I do always have fun with you."

"Of course, you do." Hayley pretended to fluff her hair.

Olivia laughed. The clouds lifted a little for the first time since she had read Peter's letter. "Thank you for helping me."

Hayley grabbed a bar napkin and a pen and handed them to Olivia. "Of course! Ok, so what do we do now? Should we make a list of your tricks and figure out which ones we're going to do?"

"Yes, that is a good first step. Then we need to go to the theatre and pull out the tricks to practice. We're going to need to go through my costumes too, and see which ones fit you."

"Oh goody! I love your costumes. You know that there isn't anything I like better than sequins and feathers."

Olivia wrote down a list of the tricks she thought they might be able to pull off.

"We need to plan out the order of the show. I guess we can still open with Chico. I did that trick all by myself, anyway. But what are we going to do when I need to change costumes? I can't have them close the curtain and have nothing going on while I'm gone for a couple of minutes."

"True, that would be pretty boring for the audience. I have an idea. Chico loves singing with me. Maybe he and I can sing a song together while you're getting ready for the next trick."

"That's a great idea! I love it. And Chico will totally love it. He adores you and loves singing with you."

"He and I sing together all the time anyway, so it won't take too much practice to add that to the act."

Olivia breathed a sigh of relief. They might actually make this work.

"Ok, let's head backstage and pull out the illusions."

They walked down to the theatre, dodging passengers leaving the Bon Voyage party. In front of the theatre, they passed the bulletin board with pictures of the headlining entertainers and the production show cast. Olivia looked at the picture of her and Peter. She glared at his smiling face. She made a mental note that she and Hayley would need to get new pictures taken for the board.

The assistant cruise director's voice boomed over the sound system. 'Not after, but B4.'

There was a smattering of laughter from the audience.

Olivia turned toward Hayley. "Ugh, they're doing Bingo. We can't use the stage until they're done."

Nigel lifted a bingo ball in the air. "Sexy legs, B11!"

An audience member shouted 'Bingo!' to a mixture of cheers and groans as the audience realized they hadn't won that round of Bingo.

"Let's go into the dressing room and go through the costumes. Maybe we can get our pictures taken together for the bulletin board in front of the theatre."
"Yeah, I think that is what we're going to have to do."

Olivia looked at the daily schedule tacked to the bulletin board. "The theatre looks like it is busy for most of the rest of the day. We'll have to come back and rehearse tonight after the show when the stage is empty."

They walked down the side aisle and parted the heavy velvet curtains, slipping backstage.

Olivia and Hayley made their way through the dark wings of the stage back to the dressing room. The dull black flooring dampened their steps.

Hayley pulled aside the curtain and sat on a stool in front of the dressing room counter and fixed her hair in the mirror.

Olivia pulled out the rack with her costumes on it. "Which costume do you want to wear for the picture?"

Hayley went through them, pushing each hanger to the side. "Oh! This one! I want to dress up like a sexy disco ball!"

"That's the dress I use for the Zig Zag Lady, but yeah, I guess it looks a little like a disco ball. If you are going to wear that, I'll wear my levitation costume. It isn't as sparkly as that dress, but it will look good with it for the picture. Let's get dressed and do hair and makeup and then head up to the photography studio. We can see if we can get Martin to take our picture now. He is probably printing the embarkation photos. Let's hope he'll agree to take our pictures for us."

"Why wouldn't he?"

"I don't think I'm his favorite person. He was yelling at my cabin steward this afternoon and I butted in. Martin didn't like that."

"He yelled at Joseph? Joseph is the sweetest guy."

"Right? Maybe I should have minded my business," Olivia said. "Now I have to ask a favor from him."

"Don't worry, I'll ask him. He won't say no to me. What man ever says no to a girl dressed up like a disco ball?" Hayley laughed and spun around, sending holographic flashes of light all over the walls. "I'm so sparkly, he might not even notice you are with me!"

The girls left through the backstage door and walked down the crew passageway. The crew members went about their work, ignoring Hayley and Olivia in their sparkling costumes.

They popped out of the crew door by the art gallery.

Katryna, the art gallery manager, was showing a passenger a huge oil painting perched on an easel by her desk. She looked up at Olivia and Hayley and smiled at them as they walked past the art gallery to the photography studio.

The only photos on the gallery walls were the stock pictures of the ship. None of the passenger photos were up yet.

"Do you think Martin's here?"

"I would think so. He had a huge line of people he was taking pictures of this afternoon. I would think he'd be printing them so the passengers can buy them after dinner tonight."

They heard low voices coming from behind a door at the back of the gallery.

Hayley walked towards the door and lifted her hand to knock. The door pushed open towards her and a crew member pushed past her, almost knocking her over.

"Excuse me. I didn't see you there." He backed up letting Hayley pass. "Martin, you have company."

"I can see that. She's hard to miss," said Martin as he leaned on the door frame, looking at Hayley. The studio lights caught the sequins on her dress, sending flashes of rainbows all around the room. He scanned Hayley from her feet, up her body, pausing longer in some places than felt comfortable, before looking at her face. "What brings you to my studio? Do I have an appointment set up with you I have forgotten? Not that I can imagine forgetting any appointment I had with you."

Hayley looked over her shoulder at Olivia and rolled her eyes. Hayley's copper colored hair, green eyes, and curvy figure drew a lot of attention. She was used to men flirting with her.

"How sweet of you. I'm Hayley. No, you haven't forgotten an appointment with me. But I do need your services."

"And which services would that be?"

"Well, you are a photographer, correct? I desperately need new photos for the show board."

"I'm happy to help you with your desperate needs." Martin leered.

Hayley pretended she didn't understand his meaning and gestured towards Olivia. "My friend and I are so grateful for your help."

Martin turned and looked at Olivia. "Oh, you."

"Oh! You know my friend. How wonderful," Hayley said, intentionally ignoring Martin's obvious dislike of Olivia. "Olivia and I need our pictures taken. We were hoping you could fit us in."

Martin looked like he was about to say no to Olivia, but he glanced at Hayley.

Hayley spun around under the studio lights. "Oh my, your beautiful lighting makes me feel like a diamond."

"I guess I can fit you in. Maybe after, you and I could go out to dinner?" Martin looked at Hayley.

"That would be lovely, and I'd love to take you up on your offer, but not tonight. Olivia and I have to rehearse our new act. That's why we need you to take our picture. We're starting an act together." Hayley cocked her head. "But, another night?"

Martin walked over, grabbed his camera, and put the strap around his neck. "Why don't you stand here, Hayley." He put his hand on the small of Hayley's back and moved her toward the backdrop. "And you can stand here." He gestured towards Olivia, putting her behind Hayley, half in shadow.

"Olivia. I need you up next to me, in these pretty studio lights." Hayley grabbed Olivia and pulled her up next to her.

Olivia's pleasant expression slipped into annoyance.

Hayley took Olivia's hand and pulled her close, whispering in her ear. "Smile, my friend. Just ignore him."

Hayley made a silly face at Olivia. She couldn't help but laugh at her friend. They posed, following Martin's suggestions for how to stand. Despite what a jerk he was, he knew his stuff as a photographer.

"Hayley, come back tonight around 8 and pick up your images."

"Sounds lovely. I can't wait."

They practically raced out of the studio. The door to the crew hallway shut behind them with a thunk.

"What a creep" Olivia put her hands on her hips. "I'm dreading having to go back there to pick up the pictures from him"

"I've handled worse than him." Hayley shrugged. "Don't worry. I'll deal with it."

After they were out of their costumes and back in their street clothes, Olivia suggest they go to her cabin. "We can check on Chico. Maybe you two can practice your duets."

Hayley put her hand up to her chin. "Do you think Chico would like to sing a jazzy little number, or maybe have a rap battle with me?"

Olivia unlocked her cabin door and pushed it open.

"Hey, hottie! What are you doing?"

"Chico! Stop calling Hayley 'hottie'! You silly bird." Olivia crossed her arms. " At least he didn't wolf whistle when he saw you this time."

"Chico can call me hottie or whistle at me any time. He knows how much I adore him. He can get away with just about anything, as far as I'm concerned."

Hayley sang a scale, and Chico followed along. Hayley stopped singing at the end of the scale, but Chico launched himself into jazz scatting with his best Ethel Merman impression.

Hayley laughed and gave him a couple of treats. She started a new song, but Chico just looked at her while he was eating his treat.

"Give him one at a time or you won't be able to get him to sing with you because he'll be too busy eating." Olivia got out a couple of sunflower seeds and put the treat bag in the desk drawer. "That boy is completely food motivated. There is nothing more embarrassing than being onstage with him and he ignores you because he's too busy eating to perform."

Hayley waited for him to finish his seeds and sang to Chico.

Chico joined in, belting out the chorus at the top of his voice.

"Shh! Silly birdie, you are being too loud."

Chico cocked his head at Hayley and paused for a second. He squawked loudly, "Quiet!"

"Yeah, right idea, wrong execution!"

Chico lowered his head so Hayley could give his neck feathers scratches. He purred like a cat.

Hayley giggled. "He's such a character."

"He sure is."

Hayley launched into another song, and Chico danced to the rhythm before picking up a couple of the words. "I guess we'll need to work on that one. Although, he is pretty cute when he dances, too"

Hayley sang his favorite song again. Chico bobbed up and down while he sang along.

Hayley sighed. "I am all sung out. Olivia, let's get something to eat. Do you want to go to the buffet on the Lido deck or the Officer's mess? I'm starving."

"I'm hungry too. Lunch seems like a lifetime ago." Olivia shivered. "Everything has changed since then."

"Yes, everything has changed. But, it has changed for the better. You'll see."

Olivia sighed. "I hope so."

Hayley put Chico on his perch. "How about the buffet? It'll be quiet up there since most of the passengers will eat in the dining room on the first night."

Olivia remembered that the buffet had her favorite dessert on the first night of the cruise. "Sounds good. They have chocolate cake on the desert buffet tonight. I could really use some chocolate cake. A day like today screams for chocolate cake."

Chico chimed in, "Mmmm, cake!"

Olivia shook her head. "Not for you buddy, chocolate isn't good for birdies."

Chico harrumphed.

"We'll get my favorite duet partner some blueberries and mango, I promise."

"No wonder he likes you so much, Hayley. You sing with him and you remember his favorite fruits!"

"He's adorable." Hayley looked at the clock. "Oh shoot, it's almost 8. Martin said to pick up the pictures from him at 8. I'll go pick up the pictures and meet you at the buffet."

"Ugh. I'll go pick them up. I don't think you should have to deal with Martin after how badly he behaved with you."

Hayley waved her hand. "Don't worry. I can handle him. You're the one who really got on his bad side."

"Do you actually think he has a good side?"

"That's a fair point." Hayley grinned. "I'll be fine getting the pictures alone. I can handle an obnoxious photographer."

"Ok, if you're sure. I'll get Chico settled, and then I'll meet you up at the buffet on Lido deck."

"Sounds like a plan. Having plans to meet someone for dinner will be a good excuse to just grab the pictures and go."

Olivia turned on the tv to keep Chico company. He'd already tucked one foot up into his feathers and his eyes were half closed. All the singing and snacks had worn him out. Olivia heard him crooning to himself as she closed her cabin door.

Olivia fixed a salad so she wouldn't feel guilty about eating her chocolate cake. One of the hardest parts of working on a cruise ship was constantly being surrounded by so much amazing food. She needed to fit in her costumes, and in the tricks. She had to be careful not to go overboard with the ship's food, no matter how good it tasted.

Olivia picked a table in the back, overlooking the wake of the ship. She pulled her book out of her pocket and read while she ate.

"Sorry, I took so long." Hayley put down her tray and sat across from Olivia.

"Did Martin give you trouble? I knew I shouldn't let you go by yourself."

"No, actually, he wasn't even there. I waited in the studio for a couple of minutes, figuring he would show up. He wasn't anywhere around. I didn't want you waiting for me for too long, so I figured I'd try again after dinner."

"Bummer that you didn't get the pictures."

Hayley dug into her chicken satay and veggies.

A waiter came by and she ordered them each a glass of wine.

Hayley lifted her glass to Olivia. "Cheers."

Olivia took a sip of the wine and felt warmth wash over her. "That was a good idea. It's been such a stressful day and we have a long night ahead of us."

Hayley took a sip and leaned back in her chair. "That hit the spot."

They finished their dinner and their wine. Olivia went up to the buffet and got their chocolate cake and coffee. It was going to be a late night of rehearsing, so a little sugar and caffeine were a necessity.

"I'm glad you talked me into getting that chocolate cake. It was so good." Hayley pushed back her empty plate and let out a satisfied groan. "It's weird that Martin wasn't there when he'd told me to come get the pictures tonight at 8"

Olivia licked her fork. "I hope they turned out. I don't want to have to ask him to redo the pictures."

"I'm sure we'll get at least one picture we can use."

Olivia shook her head. "The more I think about it, the more I don't think it is a good idea for you to deal with him alone. I'll go with you. If I'm there, he won't cross any lines."

"I'm sure I would be fine, but we'll go together if it makes you feel better. Stay quiet so you don't rile him up."

Olivia turned at the sound of a familiar British accent. The cruise director, Tristan Waterson, walked into the buffet with a man in a white purser uniform. Tristan wore his evening cruise staff uniform, a blue blazer with gold trim on the cuffs, and white pants.

Olivia sighed.

Hayley followed her gaze. "Mmmm. Yeah, he's definitely a head turner."

Olivia shook her head and shrugged. "He didn't turn my head."

"Olivia, if your head had turned any harder, you wouldn't need the illusion to do the Zig Zag Lady. Your head would already be off your body. Don't worry, everyone looks at him like that." Hayley sighed. "The accent, the blue eyes, the blond hair. Did I mention his accent? How could that not catch your attention? He's got my attention."

Olivia rolled her eyes.

Hayley turned to get a better look. "That new purser, Blake, isn't too bad to look at either. I met him when I stopped to visit with Sophie at the Purser's desk. One of the best perks of this job is all the good looking men who work on ships." Hayley wiggled her eyebrows, making Olivia laugh.

"You can look at men like that. You're single. I'm..." Olivia paused midway through the sentence. "Oh. I was going to say that I am in a relationship, but I guess I'm not."

"Peter was an idiot to let you go. Every single guy on this ship is going to be making moves on you as soon as they find out you are single."

"I'm not interested in dating. I can't even wrap my head around being single right now." Olivia looked towards the table where Tristan and Blake were eating their dinner. "We just need to get through the show."

"For someone not interested in men, you sure can't keep your eyes off of our handsome cruise director."

"I wasn't looking at Tristan because he's handsome."

Hayley lifted one eyebrow and looked at Olivia questioningly.

"Ok, yes, he's very good looking. But, I was thinking about having to fess up that Peter is gone and that we're going to try to do the show without him. I am dreading that conversation."

Hayley forced her gaze away from Tristan and back towards Olivia. "We're not going to 'try' to do the show. We are going to do the show. Why would you tell him about Peter leaving?"

"Why wouldn't I tell him? He's the cruise director and my boss. Your boss, too, for that matter. Of course, I have to tell him."

Hayley leaned in towards Olivia. "Have you ever heard the phrase 'It's better to ask for forgiveness than permission?'"

"That might be what you would do, but that is just not who I am." Olivia threw herself back in her chair. "I follow the rules."

An announcement came over the speaker system. "Operation Bright Star, 9, aft, port; Operation Bright Star, 9, aft, port."

Tristan's head jerked up. He excused himself from his dinner companion and raced out of the dining room.

"Well, I guess telling Tristan is out of the question right now, since he took off like there was an iceberg straight ahead."

Olivia wrinkled her nose. "You're right. I can't tell him now. I'll catch up with him later. Now, let's go pick up the pictures from Martin. I'll need to take

Chico his birdie bag after. It's been an hour since he last ate. I am sure he is starving to death after his nap."

Officers and crew members filled the passageway in front of the photography studio. Tristan's blonde head peaked above the crowd.

Olivia nudged Hayley. "This must have been why he raced off when that announcement had come on."

A crew member walked up and stepped in front of them. "Excuse me. This portion of the ship is closed to passengers."

"We're not passengers, we're entertainers. We're picking up the pictures Martin took of us."

"I'm afraid that won't be possible." He crossed his arms and shook his head. "This area is closed."

"It'll only take a minute. Martin told us to stop by and pick up the pictures." Hayley walked forward. "We'll pop in and out. We'll stay out of everyone's way."

He put his arm out, stopping them. "Ma'am, as I said, this area is closed."

"How long until it reopens?"

"I need you and your friend to leave."

"We can go wait in the art gallery until we can get our pictures." Olivia grabbed Hayley's arm and pulled her back towards the gallery.

The gallery was empty of passengers.

Katryna was talking to an officer.

Olivia caught Katryna's eye and waved, but Katryna turned her back, leaned in closer to the officer, and said something to him. He glanced at Hayley and Olivia and headed towards them.

"Victor, I will handle this from here."

"Yes, sir."

"Ms. Morgan. Ms. Fensby. I'm Security Officer Ballas, I need to speak with Ms. Fensby. Please, come this way."

"Speak to me about what? I don't have a lot of time. We need to get our photographs and get to our rehearsal."

"Ma'am, I asked you to follow me." He reached towards Hayley and took her arm in his hand. He walked down the passage, pulling her with him.

Olivia reached for Hayley and grabbed her arm back from the security officer. "What are you doing? Get your hands off of her. She's not going anywhere with you."

"Ms. Morgan, let Ms. Fensby's hand go. She is going with me. We have a witness who reported Ms. Fensby fighting with the victim just before he was found dead."

"What? Wait, victim? Who is dead?"

4

Officer Ballas paused and turned towards Hayley. "Ms. Fensby, did you go to the photography studio earlier this evening?"

"Yes. I did, but no one was there. Are you saying Martin is dead?" Hayley backed away. "I didn't fight with him. I haven't even seen him since he took our pictures hours ago."

"There is a witness who saw you go to the studio. She heard arguing a little while later."

"I went to the studio, but Martin wasn't there. I left and went to dinner, but I didn't argue with him."

"Well, a witness has reported otherwise."

Olivia looked over at Katryna and caught her eye. Katryna looked away. "This witness is telling you she saw Hayley go in the studio and that later she heard arguing, right? That doesn't mean that Hayley was the person arguing."

"I don't need suggestions on how to do my work," Officer Ballas barked. "Ms. Fensby, Follow me."

Officer Ballas grabbed Hayley's arm again and lead her to a small office. Olivia walked in right behind them.

The officer turned and looked at Olivia. "You can wait outside, Ms. Morgan. You are not involved in this."

"Yes, I am involved in this. Hayley is my friend."

Olivia could see the anger rising in Officer Ballas. His dark eyes looked at her like lasers. He took a threatening step towards her.

Olivia took a step back, stiffened her back, and stood up straighter. She would not let herself be intimidated.

Hayley put her hand on Olivia's arm and looked at her pleadingly. Under her breath she whispered, "Don't make this worse. I can handle him."

Hayley raised her voice so Officer Ballas could hear. "I'll be ok, I didn't do anything wrong. I'll be fine with speaking with the officer."

"Fine, but I will be right outside the door if you feel you need a witness." Olivia glared at Officer Ballas as she shut the door behind her.

She put her ear against the wall, trying to hear what they were saying in the office.

She could barely make out Officer Ballas's deep rumble of speech. Hayley's higher pitched voice was easier to discern, but she still couldn't make out many words.

"Are you waiting to see the security officer, too?"

Olivia jumped and looked at the man behind her.

She sighed relief at the cabin steward uniform. She'd thought an officer was coming to yell at her for eavesdropping.

"No, Joseph, I'm not waiting to see the officer. I'm waiting for my friend to be done talking to him."

"Oh, I thought he might have wanted to talk to you about what happened between me and the photographer this afternoon. That bully reported me to my boss. I might lose my contract and get sent home."

"Oh no, I'm sorry he did that. I had hoped he'd drop it since it did not hurt his camera."

"I have kids to feed. We need the money from this contract to take care of them and my parents. I was hoping I could talk to my supervisor and explain. Then I got a message to come speak to Officer Ballas."

Joseph clenched his jaw. "I'll make Martin pay for doing this to me. I can't lose this job."

Olivia's eyes widened. "Joseph, I need to tell you something."

The office door opened.

"I'll get back to you if I have more questions." Officer Ballas escorted Hayley out of his office. "Joseph, come in. Take a seat."

Olivia touched Joseph's arm and said his name.

Officer Ballas glared at her. He motioned for Joseph to come in the office and slammed the door shut behind them.

Hayley leaned against the wall, her head hanging down.

"Oh Hayley, are you ok?" Olivia put her arm around her friend's shoulders as they walked away.

"I've been better. What if he really thinks I could have murdered Martin?" Hayley shivered. "What if he doesn't find the actual killer?"

"We will not let that happen. I knew I should have gone with you to the studio."

"You couldn't have known that Martin would get killed and that I'd be a suspect."

"No, but if I had followed my instincts and gone with you, you would have had a witness that Martin wasn't even there."

Hayley took Olivia's hands in hers. "Or we'd both be suspects."

Olivia shuddered. "If anyone should be a suspect, it is me. I was so angry with him for how he treated Joseph and you. You handled him like a champ and hardly even got annoyed with him when he was acting like such a creep towards you."

"Well, don't tell Officer Ballas you should be a suspect." Hayley opened the crew door. "We don't need him going after you, too."

"Hopefully, he'll figure out who did this quickly. We know you didn't do it, so he'll have to figure out that someone else did it, eventually."

Olivia followed Hayley down the stairs. "You aren't the only one he's looking at. He called Joseph up to talk to him about their confrontation at embarkation."

"Are you sure that's why he wanted to talk to Joseph?" Hayley asked.

"That's what Joseph said. Martin reported his side of the story to Joseph's supervisor and Joseph got in trouble. He's afraid that he's going to lose his contract and get sent home."

"That would stink."

"I was going to tell Joseph what happened to Martin, but then you came out. He was telling me he wanted Martin to pay because he got him in trouble. I hope he doesn't say that to Officer Ballas. This is awful. I know neither of you did anything to Martin." Olivia exhaled. "What did Officer Ballas ask you?"

"He wanted me to tell him everything I did from when I got on the ship this afternoon until he saw me in the passageway with you in front of the art gallery. I told him I hadn't seen Martin when I went to the studio to pick up the pictures and that I didn't argue with him." Hayley shrugged. "But I don't have any proof. No one saw me come out of the studio. I wish I knew who he'd fought with."

"Officer Ballas will have to figure out who was arguing with Martin."

"Only if he believes me." Hayley's hands were shaking.

"Even if he doesn't believe you, it is his duty to investigate and try to figure it out for sure."

"Well, for now, all we can do is go practice the act. I don't want to let you down at the show."

Olivia took her friend's hand in hers. "With this going on, I wouldn't blame you if you want to bail on the magic show."

"No, I made a promise to you I would do it with you. Plus, it'll take my mind off of all of this."

Olivia gave Hayley a hug. She realized she still had Chico's birdie bag in her hand. "Would you mind if we stopped at my cabin to give Chico his goodies? We can go backstage and pull out an illusion to practice after."

"You know I am always okay with visiting my little green duet partner. I love it when he eats blueberries and his beak looks like he's got purple lipstick on. I need a laugh from that silly critter."

Within 15 minutes, Hayley and Olivia had fed Chico and headed backstage. They pulled out the biggest case and unpacked the trick.

Olivia knelt on the stage.

Hayley watched Olivia quickly assemble the illusion. "I guess I'm going to have to know how these tricks work now that I'm part of the show. That stinks. I liked not knowing. I've always loved magic tricks."

Olivia sat back on her heels and looked questioningly at Hayley. "Really? I have never really liked magic. Ironic, right? I never watched it when I was a kid or wanted a magician for my birthday party. I only started doing it because Peter needed an assistant. And now, here I am, a magician, doing my own magic show. How weird is that?"

"So, if you didn't want to be a magician, what did you want to be when you grew up? This might be your opportunity to try something else."

Olivia thought for a second. "I'm already grown up. Feels kind of late to decide what I want to be.'

"Well, you don't have to be a magician if you don't want. Once Tristan can get a replacement act, you could get off of ships and do something else."

"I don't even know what I would do. I've been following Peter's dream for so long I haven't even thought about mine."

"What did you like to do when you were a kid?" Hayley asked.

"I liked to read and play with my pets. Not very promising for career prospects. I doubt I can find a job that pays me to read and play with Chico." Olivia laughed. "What about you? Did you know you were going to be an entertainer when you were little?"

"Sort of. I've always loved to sing. My mom said that I came out of the womb singing and dancing. It's the only thing I ever wanted to do for a living. And I love to travel and see the world. Working on ships gives me the chance to sing, dance and get paid to travel." Hayley looked around the stage and smiled. "It's the perfect job for me, but it might not be the perfect job for you."

"When I was in school, I used to get sick to my stomach if I had to do any public speaking or sing in front of people." Olivia laughed. "Never thought I would end up a performer."

"As hard as this is, you have an opportunity to try something new. Something that makes you happy. If you could do anything, what would that be?"

"I love animals more than anything. I've always been an animal person. That's part of why we got Chico for the show. I was so lonely without a pet. Peter said that I could get an animal as long as I trained it to do something entertaining, so it could go in the show." Olivia's face lit up. "One day I was in a pet store visiting all the animals there and I heard someone singing this dramatic song in the back of the store. I went back to see who was singing and this green and yellow parrot was singing like an opera singer."

"Chico!"

"Yes! When he saw me he stopped singing and said 'What you looking at?' I laughed so hard, I knew he was the perfect addition to the show. He could sing like an angel and he had a sense of humor."

Hayley reached down to help Olivia pick up a long piece of flat black metal. "So working with Chico makes you happy? What about a job working with parrots?"

"I don't even know what kind of job that would be." Olivia looked down at the prop in front of her. "I can't even think about my future right now. We need to get through this cruise. They'll fire me if I can't make this show work. It feels so overwhelming. I've never done a show by myself. Why am I even trying to do it alone? I should just tell Tristan what happened and let him kick me off the ship when we get to Nassau."

"You aren't alone. You have me and Chico. Don't underestimate yourself. You have been a part of this act for years. You are going to be amazing at it and

Tristan will want to extend your contract because the passengers will love your show so much."

"I hope you are right. Ok, I have this together. Are you ready to fly?"

Hayley looked at Olivia. "Whoa, wait, I thought you were going to fly, not me."

"We don't have time for me to teach you and Chico how to do his part of this trick together. I know how to do it and he's used to me. It's one less thing to change in the show. You are going to need to do this part of the trick. It's easy, all you have to do is lay there. Don't worry."

Hayley looked at the levitation and back at Olivia. "I have to make a confession. I'm afraid of heights. There is no way I can do that trick."

"I've never seen you scared of anything. You are the bravest person I know."

"I know it is dumb, but I can't help it. I am terrified of heights." Hayley looked at the trick and shuddered. "There is no way I am going up there. Can't I do the part with Chico and you do this trick?"

"There is a lot more to Chico's part than it looks. It took me months to learn how to produce Chico out of thin air without anyone seeing what I'm doing.

Your part of the levitation mostly requires strong abs. Which you already have."

Hayley looked at the trick again and sighed. "What have I gotten myself into?"

The sound of waves hitting her porthole slowly pulled Olivia up from the depths of sleep. The rocking of the ship always lulled her into a deeper sleep than she ever got on land.

She looked at the clock on the desk. She'd slept through breakfast.

She and Hayley had rehearsed until almost 3 am. The sea had kicked up waves, making the stage roll. Hayley had been trying to practice the levitation, but the enormous waves had been too much for her. Every time she'd gotten more than a couple of feet above the stage, she'd panicked and Olivia had to lower her back down.

They planned to rehearse again tonight, hoping for calmer seas.

Chico slept in his blanket covered cage.

Her tiny cabin seemed quiet without Peter. The low hum of tension she had felt whenever Peter was around the past few months was gone. She hadn't even realized it was there.

If she could pull off the show with Hayley, things might be better than they had been for a long time. She hoped Hayley could get her fear of heights under control.

Of course, Hayley could only do the show if they did not haul her off for Martin's murder.

Olivia turned over and covered her head with her pillow. She wasn't ready for this day to start. Since she'd already missed breakfast, maybe she could nap until the lunch buffet.

"Hello. Bird. Pretty bird. What a pretty bird." Chico quietly mumbled to himself.

Olivia lifted the pillow off her head and made eye contact with the little parrot eye peaking at her out of the hole he'd chewed in his cage cover.

He must have heard her moving around and it had woken him up.

"La, la, la, la, Laaaa!!" He trilled up the scale.

Once he was awake, he usually wouldn't go back to sleep. She lay quietly, not moving, hoping she could have a few more minutes of quiet to figure out what she needed to do today before she climbed out of bed and faced it.

Yesterday she'd been so excited to wake up. A home port day gave her a chance to catch up on errands and do a little of the regular life stuff that still needed to get done when you lived on a cruise ship. Cruise ship life looked like a full-time vacation, but it wasn't all glamorous. Sometimes you needed parrot pellets and new underwear. Olivia looked forward to days when she could run errands like a normal person.

Peter had still been asleep when she'd quietly gotten out of bed and taken a quick shower. She felt stupid that she'd been trying to keep from waking him up when he'd probably been tired from planning how he was going to leave her.

Her anger escaped her body in an exasperated sigh.

"Ooh, La la! Zip, zip, Zipadee!"

"Ok, Chico man, I'll get you uncovered. Apparently, it is birdie wake up time. I am not doing myself any favors anyway, laying here thinking about my troubles."

"Snack?"

"Yeah, I'll get your breakfast."

"Mmmmm!" Chico made yummy noises and spun around excitedly on his perch in anticipation of his breakfast.

Olivia opened his cage door.

Chico hooked his beak on the wire above the door and hauled himself out of his cage and up to the perch Olivia had bolted on top. There wasn't enough room in her small cabin for a separate play gym, but he loved hanging out on his perch, looking out the porthole at the water racing by.

She filled his cup with his parrot pellets and hopped in the shower. The tiny shower made shaving her legs a challenge, especially on days like today when the ocean was tossing the enormous ship around. Olivia was so used to the motion of the waves after all the years she'd worked on ships, she almost didn't notice it anymore. At least not until the shower curtain moved with the ship and attached itself to her backside. She peeled the shower curtain off of herself and tried to place it where it wouldn't stick to her again. She couldn't put it outside the shower or water would get all over the floor of the tiny bathroom.

As she put on her sundress and dried her hair, she couldn't stop wondering who Katryna had heard arguing with Martin.

It wasn't Hayley, so it had to be someone else. Who would have a reason to argue with Martin?

She wished that would narrow down the list, but he was such a jerk it didn't eliminate many people, especially women, who she could see yelling at him.

If Hayley hadn't handled him with the ease she had, Olivia could have easily yelled at him.

Maybe if she talked to Katryna, she would get a clue that would help her figure out who it was.

She jogged up the flights of stairs to the art gallery, pausing after a couple of floors to catch her breath before continuing to the art gallery.

Katryna was talking to a passenger about a painting in her collection when Olivia walked in. Her face was covered by the curtain of her dark hair, styled in a bob. She turned expectantly to greet her when she entered the gallery, but her smile faded quickly when she realized it was Olivia. She turned back towards her guest.

Olivia slowly walked through the gallery, looking at the paintings, waiting for the passenger to make his purchase and head out.

As he walked out of the gallery, Katryna walked up to Olivia. "Look, I don't need any trouble. I already lost half a day of commissions because they closed my gallery yesterday. If any of my customers knew that there had been a murder next door, they wouldn't want to walk through my gallery."

"I'm not here to give you trouble. I just wanted to ask you a couple of questions."

"I don't have anything to tell you."

"Please. I know Hayley didn't kill Martin. I need to figure out who was arguing with him, so she won't be a suspect anymore."

"Like I said, I don't know anything. The gallery was busy. I wasn't paying that much attention. I looked up when Hayley was walking by and waved to her. A while later, most of the people in the gallery had left to go to dinner, so it had gotten quiet. I heard arguing, a man and a woman. I've already told all of this to Officer Ballas."

"But you might have heard or seen something that you didn't even realize you had heard. If we go through it step by step, maybe you will remember something that will be a clue to who was arguing."

"Fine, I'll try to think. But if I get any customers, you have to leave."

"That's fair. Did you see anyone other than Hayley around the gallery?"

"It was hectic in here. You know how the first night of the cruise is. There were people all over. The crew door is right in front of the gallery, but Hayley is the only woman I saw come out of it. The only reason I noticed Hayley is because she waved to me when she went by."

Ok, so how long after you saw Hayley did you hear arguing?"

"I don't know. Not long. Maybe 15 minutes. Every-one cleared out for second seating at 8:15, so it must have been after that." Katryna kept looking at the door, checking for guests coming into the gallery.

"See! That is important information. Hayley was at the buffet on the Lido deck by 8:15, so it couldn't have been her. Not that I thought it could be. You heard fighting. Who was yelling? Martin or the woman? Were they both yelling at each other?"

"Mostly the woman was yelling. Her voice kept getting louder and louder."

"Could you tell what the fight was about?"

Katryna tipped her head back and looked up at the ceiling. "I heard the girl say something about her pictures. But that could be anyone since Martin was a photographer."

"Ok, but what did she say about the pictures?"

Katryna bit her lip and her eyes darted back and forth. "I honestly didn't pay that much attention. It mostly annoyed me they were fighting. It wouldn't be good for my business if they didn't stop. I heard the girl say something about her portfolio. I could hear a man's voice answer her, but not what he said. My phone rang and by the time I got off, it was quiet in the studio. I didn't think about it again until Officer Ballas told me that someone had strangled Martin."

"Strangled?"

"Yes, that's what he told me. I figured you knew." Katryna shrugged. "Yeah, he was strangled with his camera strap."

Olivia shuddered. "What a horrible way to go."

Katryna's eyes jerked towards the door. She stepped back.

Olivia turned to see what had startled Katryna and found herself looking right into the fierce espresso brown eyes of Officer Ballas.

"Ms. Morgan, looking for a painting?"

"No, I was just hanging out, talking with Katryna."

"About art?"

"Well, not exactly."

Officer Ballas crossed his arms and leaned against the gallery wall. "Miss Morgan, as I said last night. None of this is your business."

A passenger came in. Katryna looked nervously at the pair. She walked away to greet her potential customer.

"And I told you that as long as Hayley is a suspect, it is my business." Olivia took a step forward. "Plus, I learned something that could be helpful. Katryna remembered that the argument started after her customers had left for second seating. It had to be after 8:15 when they were fighting. Hayley was at the buffet by 8:15, so it couldn't have been her. Lots of people saw her at the buffet."

"Look, I was coming up to talk with Katryna. I don't need you interfering. I would have found that out when I talked to her. All without your help."

"She might not have remembered. You saw how nervous she was when you walked in."

"Lots of people are nervous around security officers. She still would have told me. I'm trained in how to question people."

"Well, now you don't have to question her because I already told you."

"I'm still going to talk to her. That is my job. I'm investigating a murder, remember? This situation is dangerous. The person who killed Martin is out there on this ship. If you go around asking questions, you could ask the wrong person and get hurt."

Olivia raised her chin and looked at him defiantly. "I can take care of myself. I really don't need you telling me what to do. Thank you very much" "

Frustration spread across his face. He took two steps towards her. "Mind your business and leave the questioning of people to me. Got it?"

Officer Ballas backed away from her as Katryna walked back over.

Olivia spun on her heals and marched out of the gallery.

The nerve of him telling her what to do.

She'd just gotten out of a relationship with someone who bossed her around. She wasn't ever going to let anyone else treat her like that again. If anything, him telling her to stay out of it made her want to figure out who had killed Martin even more.

Olivia hurried back to her cabin. She slowed as she turned the corner. Her cabin door was open.

6

She stood staring at her open cabin door. There was a flickering of light in the entrance as the person in her cabin moved around.

Olivia held her breath and took a step forward.

"Kamusta! Can you say kamusta, bird?"

"Hi! What are you doing?" Chico was happily talking with whoever was in her cabin.

She walked to the edge of the doorway and peered in.

Chico was singing a little song to the cabin steward, who was making her bed.

Olivia paused in the doorway and watched Joseph pull up the sheets and blanket, fold them down, and tuck the edges under the mattress.

Officer Ballas had interviewed Joseph. He must consider him a suspect.

She hadn't given a thought to having Joseph in her cabin before. He'd always been polite and helpful to her, but now she wondered if her instincts were wrong.

"Hey, baby!" Chico had spotted her in the doorway.

Joseph looked up to see who Chico was talking to. He gave her an exhausted half smile. "Oh, hello. Just finishing up your cabin."

Chico was dancing back and forth on his perch, asking Joseph for attention.

"What was the word you were saying to Chico? Kamusta?"

"It means hello in Filipino. I'm sorry. I won't teach him Filipino if you don't want me to."

"It's ok. I just don't want him to learn any swear words. Teaching him hello in Filipino is fine." Olivia leaned against her cabin door. "How did your talk with Officer Ballas go last night? Is everything ok?"

"I guess. He asked me what I was doing from the time Martin and I had our confrontation until I met him in his office. I told him I had delivered luggage to my cabins and then had dinner in the crew mess. After I ate, I turned down my guest's beds, like I do every night when they are at dinner. I was running a little behind because I make all my cabins a towel animal the first night of the cruise." Joseph looked down at the floor. "My supervisor came to get me to tell me that Martin had reported me for knocking over his camera and that Officer Ballas wanted to speak with me."

"Did you see your supervisor before that?"

"He is training three new cabin stewards who just joined the ship at embarkation. I don't think I saw him last night until he came to find me."

Olivia leaned against the door frame. "Did you see anyone last night? Anyone that can say you were in your cabins, not near the photography studio?"

Joseph considered her question for a moment. "I never left my cabins other than to go to the crew mess. I didn't see anyone after I got my cart ready. When I am in the cabins, I always leave the door open, so anyone who walked down the passageway would have seen me working, but I don't remember anyone specific walking by. Do you think I am in trouble?"

"I really hope not. If you think of any witnesses who saw you working, let me know, ok."

"Yes, miss. I will. I'm done with your cabin. Have a good afternoon."

"Thanks Joseph. You, too."

Chico leaned towards Joseph and flapped his wings. "Bye bye!"

"Paalam, bird." Joseph stopped and looked at Olivia. "Don't worry, it means goodbye. Maybe your bird will learn to speak Filipino?"

"Nothing Chico does would surprise me."

Joseph grabbed the used towels from the bathroom and pulled her cabin door closed behind himself.

Olivia hadn't felt nervous with Joseph in her cabin. She wasn't sure if she should trust her judgment when she had obviously been so wrong in her judgement of Peter, but Joseph seemed like a nice guy.

Chico loved it when Joseph came to clean their cabin.

Joseph was always talking to Chico or bringing him a treat.

Some of her cabin stewards had been afraid of Chico or annoyed at the extra mess he made, even though she tried to clean up after him and always tipped them well.

Joseph had been excited the first time he came into her cabin and Chico had greeted him with a melodic "Hellooo!"

The only way to know for sure that Joseph hadn't killed Martin was to find out who did.

She needed to figure out who the girl was that was fighting with Martin. Olivia's friend Sophie had worked on this ship longer than anyone else Olivia knew. She stayed on top of just about everything that happened on the ship from her spot at the Purser's desk. If she didn't know who could have fought with Martin, she would probably know someone who did.

Olivia headed up to the purser's desk to talk to Sophie.

There was a line of passengers in front of her. She deftly handled each passenger's request, easing their anxiety about whatever problem they had with her disarming 'No worries.'

Finally, the line died down and Olivia walked up to Sophie. "How can I help you? Do you need seasickness pills?"

"No, I'm fine, but thank you. Actually, I was wondering if you had heard about Martin."

"I did, mate. Can you believe it?" Sophie's eyes were wide, and she lowered her voice to a near whisper. "A murder on our little cruise ship. Who would have thought?"

"Not me, that's for sure. Hayley and I had our pictures taken by him a few hours before he was killed."

"Ah bless." Sophie shook her head solemnly. "Are you and Hayley looking to model?"

"No, why do you ask?"

"Well, I heard he had a little side business going, taking pictures of pretty crew members and helping them build a modeling portfolio."

Olivia cocked her head. "I didn't know that."

Sophie leaned in. "He did a photo shoot with one of the croupiers last week when we were at that private island. She's hoping to get off of ships and get a modeling career going. She was excited to have her portfolio started. Felt like it was going to give her a leg up. So why did you and Hayley have Martin take your pictures?"

Olivia looked around to see who was nearby. "I haven't been able to catch up with Tristan to tell him yet, so please keep this between us."

"Of course, you know I never gossip."

Sophie was a font of information, if you knew what to ask. She was in the middle of the busiest part of the ship and saw almost every passenger and crew member walk by at least once a day. Many stopped to ask her a question or say hello. Her efficient mind cataloged everyone's comings and goings, giving her lots of information about everyone on the ship.

Olivia grimaced. "Peter left me, the act, and the ship. Hayley is going to do the show with me. We were getting new photos taken to put up on the board in front of the theatre."

"Oh, my! Are you ok?"

Olivia considered if she really was ok. When she had first learned about Peter leaving, she'd been in shock. She figured that when it sunk in, she wouldn't be ok at all. They'd been together for a long time, living in a cramped cabin, working together and being together almost all the time.

"I don't really know how I feel. My entire life is upside down."

"Well, deary, I probably shouldn't say anything, but you are much better off without him."

"Do you know something I don't know?"

Sophie crossed her arms and pursed her lips. "I told you, I don't gossip."

Olivia considered questions she could ask that might prompt Sophie to tell her why she thought she'd be better off without Peter.

She opened her mouth to ask and then paused. "Maybe it is better that I don't know."

Sophie nodded. "There is that, mate."

Two of her friends had now told her she was better off without Peter. It didn't really change anything. He was gone, and she was on her own. Only time would tell if she was really better off.

"Back to Martin. Did you know him at all?"

The new Chief Purser, Blake, walked out of the office door behind Sophie.

"I'll let you know about that issue later. Is there anything else I can do to help you?" Sophie said, switching into professional mode as her new boss walked up next to her.

Olivia recognized him as Tristan's dinner companion from the buffet last night. He nodded at Sophie and Olivia as he passed. He walked down to the end of the long purser's desk to the last computer terminal and moved the mouse back and forth to bring the computer to life.

Olivia turned back towards Sophie. "You were talking about a croupier that had her picture taken. What was her name?"

"It's that pretty blonde with the long hair, Anna."

Olivia looked at the clock above the elevator. The casino wouldn't be open for a couple more hours. She really didn't want to wait until the casino opened later that day to talk to Anna. If she was the one who had fought with Martin, that would show Officer Ballas that Hayley shouldn't be a suspect.

"Do you know which cabin Anna is in? I want to ask her a couple of questions."

Blake stopped typing, turned off the monitor and walked towards them. "Sophie, who's your friend?"

"Blake, this is Olivia. She's the magic act on the ship."

"Ah, I haven't gotten to see the shows since I signed on the ship, but I will make it a point to see yours." Blake smiled a slow, lazy smile that made heat rise in Olivia's face.

"Um, I'm making some changes to the show. You might want to wait a couple of weeks until we get the kinks worked out. The revue show is tonight. It's a great show, you should go see that. My friend Hayley is the lead singer."

"That sounds lovely. I'd really like to see it. Can I take you to dinner and the show?"

Sophie let out a snort and quickly turned back towards her computer screen.

Olivia took a step back. "I don't think so. I, uh... I'm meeting a friend for dinner. But, thank you."

Blake leaned down on the wooden desk and looked right into her eyes. "How about we meet for the second show? I'll meet you in front of the theatre?"

Olivia didn't have any plans for the night until Hayley was done with the show. They couldn't get on stage until the stage crew had put away all the sets from the revue show. She'd been planning to go watch Hayley tonight, anyway. She hoped that watching her perform might give her ideas about things they could add to their show. It felt weird to tell him she wouldn't go with him and then go by herself. It would be awkward if he saw her there.

"Um, sure, I guess that is ok."

Sophie's eyes stayed glued to her computer screen, but she couldn't hide her grin.

Olivia was stunned as she turned and walked towards the elevator. Had he just asked her out on a date?

She went to shows with friends on the ship all the time.

But Blake wasn't a friend. She'd just met him.

She punched the button to call the elevator.

She stepped into the elevator.

She might have a date.

The door closed.

Olivia realized Sophie hadn't told her Anna's cabin number. She'd have to wait to talk to her when the casino opened. She couldn't open the elevator door and go back out there and ask her now.

Olivia stood in the elevator, trying to decide which button to push. Her brain couldn't focus on the numbers and what they meant. She wanted to tell Hayley about Blake asking her out, but Hayley had a run-through of the show before tonight's performance. She needed to decide where to go before someone called the elevator from in front of the purser's desk.

Sophie and Blake would see her still standing in the elevator.

Olivia jabbed at a button, and the elevator jerked into motion.

A crew member in a Hawaiian print shirt stood behind the desk in the photography studio. The gallery walls that had been empty the first night of the cruise now had pictures of smiling passengers all over them.

The crew member nodded a greeting and sat down on his stool.

A couple of passengers were walking around trying to find pictures of themselves.

Olivia walked over and looked through the pictures, but the ones Martin had taken of her and Hayley weren't there. She wondered if he had printed them.

Martin had annoyed her, but it was still awful to think of him dead.

Olivia looked around the photo gallery, trying to see where Martin might have put their pictures. Behind the guy at the desk, there was a file box with the lid tipped open.

She walked over to the wall of pictures near the desk, looking at the excited faces of the passengers.

She glanced over at the file box. Each file had a letter of the alphabet. She was trying to peek into the box when the phone rang on the desk. Olivia jumped like something had electrocuted her.

"Photo Gallery, may I help you?" The crew member wrote something on a piece of paper. "No problem, give me a few minutes and I'll have it for you."

He took the paper and went into the studio behind the gallery.

Olivia popped behind the desk and leafed through the files.

She recognized a couple of crew member's pictures. The box must be where Martin kept crew pictures. Olivia checked the "O" file, but it was empty. The only thing in 'H' file was a thick manilla envelope. Martin must have put their photos in the envelope.

Olivia hoped that was a good sign that he'd gotten a lot of shots worth printing.

Olivia picked up the yellow envelope and raced out of the studio with her head down, not wanting to see Katryna or anyone else.

She threw open her cabin door, startling Chico awake from his nap. He squawked his displeasure.

"It's all right, buddy. It's just me."

"Good night!"

"Sorry I woke you up."

"Hrumph." Chico lifted a foot, tucked it into his fluffy green breast feathers, and slowly closed his eyes.

Olivia sat down on her bed and pinched the silver tabs on the envelope together. The manilla folder was bulging with photographs.

She was excited to see if Martin had gotten any good shots they could use for the board. Olivia pulled out the stack of photos and looked at the first one. She quickly flipped through the pile.

She threw the stack of photos onto the bed.

None of the pictures were of her and Hayley.

Now, she'd need to sneak these pictures back into the studio and figure out where their pictures were.

Olivia picked the stack of photos back up and looked through them more slowly this time. There was a pretty blonde with long hair in a bikini with her back to the camera. One photo had her silhouetted against the sun. She was posing by the big rocks Olivia had seen when she'd taken the tender over to the private island last cruise. These must be the modeling shots of the croupier Sophie had mentioned.

Being a photographer was probably a good excuse for Martin to get pretty girls to let him take their pictures. At least the photos were gorgeous.

After the modeling photos were some group shots. Martin was in a few of the photos. She tried to figure out where on the ship the picture of Martin was taken. The location looked familiar, but she couldn't quite place it.

In one picture, a tuxedoed Martin was standing next to a man in a red vest. They had their arms around each other's shoulders. Their heads were leaning towards each other, almost touching. He looked familiar, but she couldn't place him. An arm with a tattoo reached in from off camera and made bunny ears behind Martin's head.

Olivia looked at the man's vest and recognized the logo from the Sea Frolic cruise line.

She flipped through the rest of the pictures.

There were a couple of pictures taken from behind of a dark-haired man sitting at a desk with stacks of cash in front of him, and a huge key ring filled with keys. A few pictures were from a snorkeling tour, taken with an underwater camera, and more of the man in the first picture in what looked like the casino cashier's office.

Other than the modeling photos, the rest of the pictures looked like snapshots, not formally posed photos.

Olivia slid most of the pictures back into the envelope, keeping out the ones she thought were of Anna. She slid her pictures into her notebook to give to her when she found her. She put the envelope in her desk drawer.

A knock on the door startled her, and Hayley burst in as soon as she opened the door. "Between our late night last night and the production show run through this morning, I am worn out and hungry. I missed breakfast. Have you had lunch yet?"

"Mmmm... lunch." Chico chimed in.

"Not you, Chico, I was asking Olivia. But I'm sure we'll bring you back some carrots."

"Snacks!"

Olivia had been so busy, she'd forgotten to get lunch. "Yes, I'm in. Lido deck?"

Over a lunch of grilled chicken with Caribbean rice, Olivia caught Hayley up on what she had learned and her 'maybe a date' to the show tonight.

"It's definitely a date." Hayley grinned. "I am jealous. Blake is dreamy,"

"Well, maybe he'll fall in love with you when he's watching you killing it on stage tonight."

"Since I'm a murder suspect, you should probably not say I might kill it on stage. Totally different meaning." Hayley shook her head.

"Sorry." Olivia shrugged. "How about 'when you bring down the house'?"

"Better."

"It feels weird to go on a date, or whatever this is. I have been in a relationship for so long, I can't imagine being with anyone other than Peter."

"If Peter came crawling back, wanting to get back together, would you?"

Olivia looked down and closed her eyes. "What Peter did was horrible, but we have so much shared history together. It feels wrong to just throw all of that away."

Hayley sighed. "Or would you just be throwing away more time?"

"Well, it isn't an option now anyway, so I guess there is no point in even trying to figure out what I would do."

Olivia pulled out her notebook and opened it up to the pictures of the blonde girl on the beach. "Any idea who this is? Sophie mentioned that Martin had taken modeling shots of Anna, the croupier."

Hayley pulled the photographs towards her. The woman's blond hair fell down her back almost meeting the top of her long, slender legs. "Yes, that's Anna. You know her. She usually wears her hair up in a bun or a braid, but I have seen her with her hair down when we went to the beach once. It was so long."

"We need to find out if she is the woman who was arguing with Martin."

Hayley's eyes widened. "You don't think she killed Martin, do you?"

"Well, someone did. Until we figure out who, you are on Officer Ballas's suspect list. We need to talk to her and find out if she was arguing with Martin. If she was, and didn't kill him, maybe she saw something that will help us find the killer."

Hayley yawned. "I was really hoping for a nap. But, you are right, I will feel better when the killer is caught, and I'm not a suspect."

They heard slot machines, clinking coins, and bells coming from the casino before they could see it. The clanking and rattling of the machines got louder, the closer they got.

The casino was surprisingly busy for the middle of the afternoon. With no windows, it was hard to tell what time of day it was once you got into the casino. A red light blinded Olivia as it spun around on top of a slot machine after a grey-haired lady in a flamingo pink pantsuit won a jackpot on a penny slot. She moved to the machine next to the one she had been using, swiped her card, and furiously pushed the button.

Hayley scanned the blackjack tables. She grabbed Olivia's hand and pulled her towards a table at the back of the casino. The croupier was fanning cards across the green felt.

Anna didn't have any guests at her table. She smiled when she caught sight of Hayley and Olivia bearing down on her. "Hello, you want to play?"

"Actually, no. We have something of yours that we thought you would want." Olivia opened her notebook and pulled out the photos of Anna on the beach, and handed them to her.

"Where did you get these?" Anna's brow furrowed. She pulled the pictures towards her chest so only the back of the photo paper showed. She looked towards the front of the casino to see if anyone was watching her and glanced up at the ceiling.

Olivia followed her gaze and saw the camera. "Sorry, I wouldn't have brought the pictures to you at work, but I didn't know where your cabin was. I thought you might want them."

"Thank you. Where did you get these?"

"They were mixed in with some other photos."

"I do, thank you." Anna stuffed the pictures under her table. Her previous smile was replaced by a strained grimace.

"The other pictures. Were they shots of me?"

"Oh no, these were the only ones we found of you. Did you hear about Martin?"

"Of course, you know gossip travels fast on ships."

Olivia had hoped Anna would mention seeing him before he'd been murdered, but she stood silently waiting for them to leave, her eyes darting towards the casino staff talking by the cashier's booth.

Olivia looked at Hayley, not sure what to do next.

"Anna, did Martin take more photos of you?"

Anna nodded, but added nothing.

Olivia decided she needed to ask Anna outright if she had argued with Martin. She obviously would volunteer nothing.

"Anna, we heard you were in the studio not long before he was killed."

"Who told you that?"

"It doesn't matter who told me. Is it true?"

Anna's eyes flashed. "What are you implying?"

"I'm not implying anything. We were curious if you saw anyone when you were there."

"Look, I don't want to get in trouble for talking at work. You'll have to excuse me." Anna turned away from them and rearranged her decks of cards.

8

The man in a casino uniform walked towards them as they were leaving the casino. Olivia recognized him. He was the crew member in the pictures with Martin.

"Ah, ladies, are you sure you can't stay a little longer and play a game of skill? Or do you prefer the slots?"

"Oh, we didn't come to play." Anna had obviously not wanted anyone to know why they'd come to see her. "We're entertainers on the ship. We often have passengers ask us questions about the amenities, including the casino, so we thought we'd stop by and check it out."

"Ah, yes, you are the girl who gets cut in two. That must be why you looked familiar. I'm Emilio, the casino manager. It would be my pleasure to give you a tour if you have a few minutes." He reached out to shake their hands.

Olivia looked questioningly at Hayley. "I have a show tonight, so I only have a few minutes, but thank you. That would be helpful."

"Are either of you gamblers?"

Olivia laughed. "No, Most casinos aren't very welcoming when they find out that I'm part of a magic act. They expect I will cheat at cards or something."

Emilio looked in surprise at Olivia. "Ah, but you are just the lovely assistant, not the magician. Why would anyone expect you to cheat at cards?"

Olivia's eyebrows shot up. She thought about picking a deck of cards up off the table and showing him what she could do with them, but didn't want to have him kick her out of the casino.

Emilio walked them through the casino, showing them different slot machines. He told them about the different card games the guests could play. Olivia could feel Anna's eyes following them as they walked.

"Thank you so much for your time, Emilio. It was great getting an insider's tour."

"My pleasure."

Olivia paused as they walked out of the casino and turned towards Emilio. "By the way, I am so sorry for the loss of your friend, Martin."

The smile on Emilio's face froze. "Excuse me?"

"I'm sorry. I assumed you had heard that Martin, the photographer, died."

"Ah yes, very tragic. I had heard." Emilio crossed his arms and leaned back on his heels. "But he was not my friend. I've seen him around the ship, of course, but that is all."

"Oh, sorry about the misunderstanding. Thanks again for the tour. We need to head out. Hayley has to get ready for her show tonight."

As they left, Olivia looked over her shoulder into the casino. Emilio and Anna were watching them.

Olivia shivered. "Wow, Anna and Emilio changed attitude towards us when we mentioned Martin, didn't they?"

"Yes, it was bananas. It was like a switch flipped. We didn't get much out of Anna. I was hoping she would tell us what she and Martin were fighting about."

"Emilio lied to us about being friends with Martin. Why would he do that?" Olivia raised her hands to her head and rubbed her temples. "He doesn't know that I have a picture of him with Martin, but the community of people who work on cruise ships is pretty small. I'm sure someone knows that they worked together on another ship and were friends. Why risk lying?"

"He's hiding something. We need to figure out what that is."

"I want you to come to my cabin and look at the picture of the two of them together. Maybe you'll see something I missed."

It took a few minutes for Chico to settle down enough from his excitement at seeing Hayley for them to get out the photographs and go through them.

Hayley slowly looked at each photo in the envelope and flipped them over to see if they had writing on the back.

Unfortunately, they were all blank. Hayley sighed and picked up the picture of Martin and Emilio again. "You are right that they are friends. The way they are leaning in towards each other with their arms around each other's backs. They look like they are having a blast together. Not something you would forget."

"Yeah, that's what I thought, too. They aren't simply co-workers posing for a picture. Do you know anyone who is friends with either of them?"

Hayley thought for a second. "I don't really know that many people who work in the casino. I knew Anna a little bit, but obviously she will not talk to us."

"No, she shut down completely."

Hayley flipped through the photos again. "We should probably take these pictures to Officer Ballas. Maybe he'll get something out of them we haven't."

Olivia grimaced. "He's made it pretty clear that he wants me to keep my nose out of the investigation. He would be livid if he knew I took these pictures."

"You didn't mean to take these. You thought you were getting our photos. Speaking of which, we still need to figure out where our photos are and get them."

"I don't want to admit to Officer Ballas that I took these. I don't want to draw his attention to us." Olivia rubbed her temples.

"Shouldn't he know that Martin and Emilio were friends? With how strangely Emilio acted when we mentioned Martin's name, he could be hiding that he killed him. We want the killer caught. We have to give them to Officer Ballas."

"I know you are right. I probably should give him the pictures." Olivia sat up straight. "Maybe when we go to the studio tomorrow to look for our pictures, we can slip the envelope back in the file box. If he's doing his job investigating, he should find it there."

"What if he has already looked through the box and the pictures were gone?"

Olivia crossed her arms. "You have your show tonight, but we'll need to deal with that tomorrow."

"You're right. I have to run. I need to get ready for the show."

Chico sang musical scales to Hayley. He wiggled his wings, begging her to pick him up.

"Not our show buddy, the revue show, but glad you are ready to sing with me."

Hayley sang a quick song with Chico and gave him a treat. "I've got to run, and you need to get ready for your date!"

"It's not a date. I am not ready to date. It is just going to watch a show with a fellow crew member." Olivia shrugged her shoulders. "I do that all the time."

"You don't go watch shows with fellow crew members who are super dreamy all the time." Hayley grinned.

Olivia slouched down in her chair. "I really don't know why I said yes. He was pretty persistent, but I should have said I was busy. I couldn't come up with an excuse fast enough."

"There is nothing wrong with going on a casual date. Peter is gone. Blake is very good looking." Hayley opened the cabin door. "Go. Enjoy a fun evening. I'll come out and say hi after the show. If you need an excuse to ditch him, you can use me as an excuse. I hope you don't though. I hope you are having so much fun you tell me to scram."

"I appreciate that. Break a leg tonight. I'll see you after the show."

After Hayley left, Olivia looked in her tiny closet. She might as well spread her clothes out into Peter's closet. No reason to have her clothes all crammed in one small closet getting wrinkled when she had the extra room to spread out.

She looked through her options of what to wear. It was formal night, so her choices were limited.

She only had a couple of formal dresses with her that weren't for the show. She tried on her short, blue cocktail dress. The beaded fringe on the hem swayed back and forth when she walked and flared out when she spun around to look in the mirror. She usually loved wearing it, but the skirt was so short she had to be careful when she crossed her legs. Olivia took it off and put it back in the closet. She tried on her floor length black satin gown. The bias cut hugged her body.

Both felt sexier than she wanted to be on this 'Not a Date.'

She settled on the black satin dress. She could cross her legs without worry and wear her flats. No one would notice her shoes under the long skirt.

At least her feet wouldn't hurt.

Olivia tucked her blonde hair back and secured it with a rhinestone clip. She threw on a coat of red lipstick, stepped back and looked at herself in the mirror.

Chico let out a loud wolf whistle.

"Glad I have your approval, Chico."

She took a deep breath and headed out the door to get something to eat before she went to the show.

It felt weird to not have anyone to go to dinner with. She was used to having Peter as her regular dinner companion. Hayley had her show, so she couldn't go with her.

She decided to grab a quick bite in the officer's mess instead of trying to navigate the other dinner options alone.

The officer's mess was mostly empty. A few people sitting at the long tables.

She grabbed a plate, looked at the options under the heat lamps. She filled up her plate and found an open seat.

She wished she'd brought a book with her.

At the other end of the mess, a chair scraped backwards and the man's low, gruff voice got louder.

She turned to see what was going on. Emilio was glaring at the woman across from him. He reached across the table and grabbed hold of her wrist. The woman pulled her hand away from him, stood up, and walked out of the mess. As she passed, Olivia realized it was Anna.

Emilio shoved his chair back and stormed out after her, leaving their half eaten meals sitting on the table.

Thankfully, they'd been so involved in their disagreement they hadn't noticed her.

Olivia quickly finished her dinner and got up to get a plate of fruit for dessert. She scooped up some melon and pineapple and turned back towards her spot.

Officer Ballas walked into the mess and picked up a plate.

She stopped in her tracks.

He scooped up some food and put it on his plate. He walked towards her and his eyes widened.

His eyes slowly followed every curve of her body, outlined by her satin dress. She felt her cheeks warm and quickly carried her fruit back to her spot at the table. She could feel his eyes on her back.

She glanced back at him. His white dress uniform emphasized his broad shoulders.

She wished she'd skipped her dessert. She stabbed a piece of melon and was just about to eat it when a plate clunked down on the table across from her.

"Mind if I join you?"

9

Her melon dangled on her fork, halfway to her mouth. She lowered it to her plate and looked up.

"Of course, Officer Ballas. But, as you can see, I am almost done with my meal. I won't be here for long."

"That's fine. Please, call me Alex."

"Ok... Alex." She paused. "I'm Olivia."

"Olivia." Her name rolled off of Alex's lips. "You look lovely tonight."

Olivia looked down at her black dress. She was used to wearing formal clothes, but she felt so vulnerable in her dress tonight. "Formal night. Of course, you know that. I'm going to see Hayley in the production show."

Olivia frowned. She regretted mentioning Hayley's name as soon as she said it.

Alex shifted uncomfortably in his seat. "Look, I'm not here to quiz you on your friend. Don't worry. I saw you sitting alone and since I am alone, I thought it would be nice to sit together."

Olivia nodded and let the breath she'd been holding go.

"I'm sorry I was short with you before." Alex pushed his plate to the side and leaned forward. "I don't want anyone else getting hurt. This is an unfortunate situation, and stressful for everyone involved. Including me. I respect that you are protective of your friend. Loyalty is a commendable trait that is in short supply in this world."

"Ain't that the truth." Olivia's lip turned up in a half smile. Peter had shaken her faith in people.

She tried to decide if she should tell him about Emilio. She wasn't sure even where to begin. "I hope you are making progress on the case."

Alex sighed. "I can't talk about it. I'm sure you understand. We have to follow protocol."

Olivia shrugged. "Ships are full of protocols. I guess I didn't think there would be a need for a protocol for murder."

"Unfortunately, there is."

Olivia glanced up at the clock. "Oh gosh! The show is going to start soon and I need to get up to the theatre."

"Of course." Alex looked at his watch. "Sorry, I didn't mean to hold you up."

"You didn't hold me up. It was good talking to you."

Olivia's shoulders dropped in relief. She didn't think Alex would have sat with her if he thought Hayley had killed Martin. She was sure he knew a lot more about what had happened than she did. Hopefully, he was close to solving the case and then she'd know for sure that Hayley was safe.

Grateful to be wearing flats, she lifted the hem of her skirt and started up the flights of stairs to the theatre.

Olivia reached the lobby in front of the theatre, her breath heavy from climbing the stairs.

Passengers in their nicest clothes milled about. The doors to the theatre were still shut.

Blake had said he'd meet her in the lobby, but she didn't see him in the crowd. Maybe she would luck out and he'd be too busy to go to the show.

The cruise staff opened the doors to the theatre. The crowd pushed through the lobby and streamed towards their seats.

Olivia felt awkward standing there waiting for Blake as the crowd thinned. She scanned the lobby one more time and walked towards the entrance.

She paused in front of the bulletin board next to the doors. The show times were written with white plastic numbers on the bulletin board's black velvet surface. A photo of the smiling cast of the show, with Hayley front and center in her glamourous costume, was pinned in the featured spot.

Olivia looked up at the picture of her and Peter tacked next to the other entertainer's pictures.

She hadn't told Tristan yet about Peter taking off. She didn't have a photo of her and Hayley to put up, and she didn't even know what she was going to do for the show.

Panic washed over her. She shouldn't even be at the show, she should be rehearsing. She turned towards the stairs to head to her cabin and almost bumped into Blake.

He smiled a slow smile at her. "You weren't going to stand me up, were you?"

"I thought you had stood me up."

"Sorry, I am late. I had a couple of things to take care of before I could get away."

"Can I take a rain check? I have a list a mile long and I really shouldn't be taking time out to go to a show."

"Ah, but we can't waste how stunning you look tonight. An hour or two won't put you too far behind. Come on, let's find a seat."

Olivia hesitated.

Blake held out his arm to her.

She paused, then tucked her hand in the crook of his elbow, and followed him into the theatre. They took their seats as the lights lowered and the pre-show music faded.

A circle of light followed Tristan as he walked center stage in front of the red velvet curtains.

Olivia couldn't concentrate on what Tristan was saying. She felt guilty that she still hadn't told him about Peter leaving. She'd feel better once she and Hayley had done a run through.

The curtains opened.

The feathers, costumes, and music carried her away. She'd seen the show before, but the spectacle always kept her attention. The first few minutes of the show were filled with color and action. Everywhere you looked, something was happening on stage, all perfectly choreographed.

The stage went dark.

The audience sat hushed, waiting for whatever came next.

Olivia leaned forward. This was her favorite part of the show. A single spotlight turned on. Hayley stood in the center of the stage in a glittery gold gown. Her copper hair glowed in the spotlight. The audience was mesmerized as she launched into her solo.

All by herself, she commanded the enormous stage. She strutted across the stage, belting into the microphone.

Being on stage was her element, for sure.

Olivia wished she was half as comfortable on stage as Hayley was.

The crowd went nuts for Hayley as she bowed and ran offstage.

Olivia grinned with pride and leaned back in her seat. She felt Blake's arm across her back, his hand next to her shoulder. She sat taller, so she didn't lean against his arm.

For the rest of the show, her body tingled with awareness of Blake sitting next to her. She sat bolt upright on the edge of her seat.

Olivia was relieved when the music built to a crashing crescendo and the confetti cannons launched sparkling metallic confetti over the audience.

A hush fell over the crowd as the curtains closed for the last time.

The audience murmured about the show and what to do next as the house lights raised. The murmur grew louder as they shuffled out of the theatre.

She turned to Blake, planning to say goodnight.

Hayley slipped out of the stage door.

A couple of the stragglers stopped her to tell her how much they'd enjoyed her performance as she came up the aisle towards Olivia and Blake. Olivia stood up to greet her friend, and Blake stood next to her.

Hayley hugged Olivia and smiled expectantly.

"Oh! Hayley. This is Blake. He's the new Chief Purser. Blake, this is my best friend, Hayley."

Blake reached out and shook Hayley's hand. "A pleasure to meet you."

"Same to you." Hayley grinned at him and then looked at Olivia and wiggled her eyebrows.

Olivia glared at her, her eyes begging Hayley to not embarrass her.

"Can I interest you two beautiful ladies in a drink?"

"Oh, I wish I could, but I am exhausted. But you and Olivia should go. Have a fun evening."

Olivia looked daggers at Hayley, but Hayley smiled at her. "Off to take my stage makeup off and head to bed."

"Then I guess it is just you and me. Shall we?" Blake put his hand on the small of Olivia's back and directed her towards the elevators. He pushed the button for the top deck and smiled at her. Passengers crowded into the elevator, pushing her closer to Blake. She could feel the heat of his hand on her back through the thin material of her dress.

He led her to a table next to the window and pulled out her chair. Her "Not-a-Date" was really feeling like a date.

"What can I get you?"

"Um, a glass of red wine?"

"Excellent."

Blake walked up to the bar to get their drinks. After he placed their order, he talked with an officer sitting at the bar.

Olivia looked out the window at the moon reflecting on the water. It was almost full. It was so beautiful. She hoped she'd be able to pull off the show and would still be on the ship next week, able to see beautiful things like the moon reflecting on the surface of the ocean.

She looked at Blake as he patted the shoulder of the officer and picked up their drinks. He turned, caught her eye, and smiled at her.

She smiled back.

Maybe a glass of wine with a handsome man would take her mind off of the show and her future.

Behind Blake, a blur of white caught her eye. The officer in his dress whites put down his empty glass, turned away from the bar, and stood up.

It was Alex.

He caught her eye and smiled. His face froze as he saw Blake hand her the glass of wine and sit down across from her.

"Olivia, we never really got to talk while we were at the show. Tell me a little about yourself."

Olivia dragged her gaze away from Alex and looked at Blake.

"Well, let's see." She looked back towards the bar, but Alex was gone. "We've worked on ships for a while."

"We?" Blake asked.

"Yes, my ex and I. Now I am doing the show with Hayley. What about you? How long have you been a purser?"

"I've worked as a purser for many years, on many ships."

Olivia felt like she'd forgotten how to do small talk. She took a sip of her wine, hoping he'd keep talking. The wine was fantastic. She took another sip and smiled at him.

"Do you like the wine I picked out for you?"

"Oh yes, it is lovely. Thank you. Did you enjoy the revue show?"

"The show was very entertaining, but the company was even better."

Olivia blushed. No one had flirted like this with her in a very long time. "Did you work with Tristan on another ship?"

"Tristan?"

"Yes, Tristan, the Cruise Director. I saw you with him at dinner right before he got called to the photography studio over Martin."

"Ah, yes, dinner with Tristan. I'm sorry I didn't notice you. I shouldn't have missed such a beautiful woman." Blake held her gaze until she looked down. "When I joined the ship, Tristan introduced himself and showed me around. He was nice enough to invite me to dinner."

"Tristan is very welcoming. Exactly the right personality for his job. It surprised me when he left midway through dinner. I had planned to come by and talk to him, but he left. We didn't know at the time about Martin."

"Very unfortunate."

"Yes, it is. Martin had taken Hayley's and my picture just a couple of hours before he was killed."

"That has to be disturbing for you. Did you know him well?"

"No, I didn't really know him at all. We hadn't gotten off on the right foot either. He didn't like me much."

Blake shook his head. "He must have been a fool to not like you."

"I know it isn't nice to speak ill of the dead, but if I'm being honest, I didn't like him much either."

Blake let out a short laugh.

"Maybe he was just having a bad day. Oh goodness. That sounds so callus. He was killed, so he sure wasn't having a good day."

Blake took a sip of his drink. "Was Sophie able to help you with your issue earlier?"

"My issue? Oh yes. Sophie is wonderful. I'm sure you'll love having her on your team."

"She's very efficient."

"She is. Anytime I need something, she always knows where to direct me. She's excellent at her job."

Blake put down his drink and looked out the window. The moonlight glistened in the wake of the ship.

"So, did you find Anna?"

10

"Anna?" Olivia crossed her arms.

"Yes, weren't you asking Sophie about her?" Blake asked.

"Yes, I was. I found her, thank you. I wanted to return something of hers that I had found."

Blake smiled. "That was nice of you. So, you said you were changing your show?"

"Yes, I wish Hayley and I had been able to rehearse tonight. We don't have that much time to get up to speed."

"I'm sure you will do a wonderful job. I can't wait to see your show. What are you changing?"

Olivia's heart skipped a beat, thinking about doing the show. She'd always followed Peter's lead during the show, and now she was going to have to be the one keeping the show moving. Olivia told Blake some of her ideas and how she was integrating Hayley and her singing and dancing, along with Chico, into the show.

"Do you think we can pull it off?"

Blake didn't answer her. He was looking past her. Olivia turned to see what had captured his attention. She looked around the lounge. The ship's pianist was playing jazzy background music over the hum of conversation. Her gaze landed on Emilio. He was sitting at a high top table, engrossed in conversation with a dark-haired woman.

"Blake?"

Blake's head jerked back towards Olivia. "My apologies. I got distracted. Please go on. You were talking about your parrot?"

Blake glanced at Emilio, then pivoted his attention back to Olivia, smiling at her.

"Do you know Emilio?" Olivia asked.

Blake looked at Olivia and cocked his head. "Yes, do you?"

"He gave Hayley and I a tour of the casino earlier."

"Stay away from him."

Olivia's muscles tensed and her eyes widened in surprise as she turned to look at Blake. "Why?"

Blake reached across the table and took her hand. "I'm sorry. I didn't mean to be so abrupt but, I don't want you to get hurt."

"Why do you think he would hurt me?"

Blake looked over at Emilio and shook his head. "Let's put it this way. You don't want to get involved with him."

"Well, thank you for the warning."

"Are you upset?" he asked.

Olivia shook her head. "No. I mean, I appreciate your concern. But I don't need you to protect me, Blake. I can take care of myself."

"I know you can."

Olivia took the last sip of her wine. It was sour on her tongue. She put down her empty glass.

"Can I get you another glass of wine or an Irish coffee?"

Olivia hesitated.

"I'm going to have an Irish coffee." Blake smiled at Olivia. "Would you like one, too?"

Olivia thought for a second. "Sure, why not?"

"Excellent." Blake went up to the bar and placed their order.

Olivia turned and looked at Emilio. He was talking with Katryna. Katryna saw Olivia looking at them and gave Olivia a strained smile.

She glanced up at Blake, but he was still at the bar, talking to the bartender. He picked up their coffees and carefully walked towards her, trying not to spill the hot coffee.

"I hope you like whipped cream."

"I do, thank you."

Olivia took a sip of her coffee. She got whipped cream on her nose. Blake reached across the table and wiped off the whipped cream with his thumb, his hand on her cheek. Her heart beat faster as he licked the whipped cream off his thumb.

Olivia forced herself to breathe. It was way too soon after her breakup with Peter to be dating another man. She hadn't even processed the breakup yet. Her time and energy needed to go towards getting her show ready.

"Blake, I..." A wave of nausea hit her. Sweat beaded on her forehead. She fanned herself with her hand, trying to cool the flush of heat that came over her.

"Are you okay?" Blake asked. "You look pale."

"I think I'm going to be sick," she said.

Blake stood up from the table. "Let's go."

"Go where?"

"We're leaving," he said. "Come on. Let's get you to your cabin."

Blake took her by the arm and led her out of the lounge.

The lounge shifted and spun.

Olivia put her hand on the wall to steady herself. Her head was spinning and she felt like she was going to faint.

Blake guided her out of the lounge and towards the elevators. Olivia stumbled and almost fell over. Blake grabbed her shoulders and held her up.

"We'll get you to your cabin and you can lie down. Do you think you are seasick?"

"No, I never get seasick. I feel awful." Another wave of nausea came over Olivia again.

"Let's get you out on deck so you can get some fresh air." Blake wrapped his arm around her shoulders and helped her through the door to the outside deck. The ocean breeze felt cool on her sweaty skin. She shivered. Blake took his jacket off and draped it around her shoulders. He pulled over a lounge chair and had her sit down.

The fresh air helped. She took a deep breath of the sea air.

Color came back into her cheeks.

Blake looked at her, nervously fidgeting with the change in his pocket. "Do you think you feel up to going to your cabin, or do you need to stay out here a little longer?"

"No, I think I am okay. I'll go to my cabin. Sorry to end the evening on such a rough note."

"Don't apologize. I'm sorry you are feeling badly. I'll walk you to your cabin and make sure you get there, okay?"

"I'm fine, really. I can get to my cabin by myself."

"I insist. I wouldn't be able to sleep tonight if I didn't know you were safely back in your cabin."

"I appreciate that. Thank you."

Blake pushed the down button on the bank of elevators. When they reached her cabin door, she turned to him and said goodnight.

He reached for her key card. "Here, let me." He swiped it and opened the door to her cabin.

"Gadzooks!" Chico squawked.

"Ah, Chico! Sorry to startle you. It's okay, buddy." Olivia sunk down onto her bed, still feeling a little wobbly. "This is my friend Blake. Blake, this is Chico."

Blake looked at her and then at the green and yellow parrot sitting on his perch, giving him the evil eye. He backed away from Chico's cage. "Uh, hi."

"Fiddlesticks!"

Blake took a step towards Chico.

"Patooey!" Chico rocked back and forth on his perch, his eyes flaring.

Olivia sighed. "That's enough Chico."

"Are you alright, Olivia? If so, I think I'll see you tomorrow."

Olivia closed her eyes and sighed. "Yes, thank you. I'm sure I'll feel better tomorrow. I appreciate you making sure I got to my cabin safely."

"Of course."

Blake practically raced out of her cabin.

"Dude! You scared him. What is wrong with you? I'm sorry we woke you up, but that kind of behavior is unacceptable."

"Bad boy! A good boy!"

"Yelling at our guests, especially one that just made sure I got back to my cabin when I wasn't feeling well, is not being a good boy."

"Humph."

Olivia collapsed back into her bunk. The crisp sheets felt soft and smelled of laundry detergent. It had been a long day and that wave of nausea had taken everything she had left. She fell asleep going over her list for the show.

Olivia woke to knocking echoing in her head. She put her pillow over her head, but the knocking kept up. Her head was pounding.

Someone was knocking on the door. She dragged herself to the door and peaked out the peephole. She pulled the door open for Hayley and climbed back into bed.

"Hello, bird, hello birdie, oh my!" Chico greeted Hayley.

Hayley pulled Chico's cover off his cage and opened the curtains in front of the porthole. She sank down at the foot of the bed. "You missed breakfast. You look awful. Have a little too much fun last night? A few too many drinks?"

"Absolutely not! I only had one glass of wine. Blake and I were in the lounge and I started feeling terrible, so we came back to my cabin."

Hayley wiggled her eyebrows at her, and her eyes flashed.

"Blake was a perfect gentleman. He made sure I got safely in my cabin and then he left. I think he was a little nervous around Chico."

"This sweet bird scared him?"

"Ah, you're used to him, but lots of people are afraid of birds. Especially birds with sharp beaks. They don't know what a gentle bird he is. You had to be nervous the first time you met him?"

"Yeah, a little I guess. But now he's my duet partner, isn't that right?" Hayley burst into song, and Chico joined in.

Olivia grabbed her bottle of water and drank about half of it while Chico and Hayley sang. The pounding in her head was fading.

"Besides Chico, there was someone that made Blake nervous last night."

"Really, who?"

"Emilio."

"Oh! Interesting. Tell me all about it."

Olivia summarized Blake's reaction to Emilio and his warning to her to stay away from him. "I really didn't like him telling me what to do. But I guess he was looking out for me. That's probably good, right?"

"Girl, he seemed pretty smitten with you when I saw you guys after the show. My guess is that he doesn't want you hanging out with any other guys."

Olivia considered her point. "No, it was more than that. He couldn't take his eyes off of Emilio. We were talking, and he kept looking past me towards him. Something about Emilio upset him."

Hayley put Chico on his perch on top of his cage and leaned back against the wall. "You found those pictures of Martin and Emilio. Emilio lied about knowing him, and now Blake is warning you to not go near him. Do you think Emilio could have had anything to do with Martin's death?"

"Something's fishy, that's for sure. It's weird. He seemed nice when he gave us the tour. I hate to think we could have been right there with Martin's murderer and not known. But he totally flipped when I mentioned Martin. It was like night and day. He must know something. He and Anna were having some kind of disagreement in the Officer's Mess when I ate dinner last night. I don't even want to say this, but do you think we should take the pictures to Alex and tell him about Emilio?"

"He will not be thrilled with you having the pictures." Hayley's cheeks ballooned out as she forcefully exhaled and rubbed the creases out of her forehead. "Oh man, I guess we have to go to him, but I gotta be honest. I'm nervous. Do you think us having the pictures is going to make him think there is more reason to believe I fought with Martin and maybe killed him?"

"I hope not. I hope us bringing him the pictures and telling him what we've learned will help him find the killer."

Olivia said goodbye to Chico and shut the door to her cabin. A door of a cabin down the hall flew open and Joseph raced out. He shot down the passageway towards his cart.

Olivia quickened her step to catch up with Hayley. "Did you see that?"

Hayley looked confused. "See what?"

"Joseph. He came out of that cabin."

"Yeah, so? He's a cabin steward. He comes out of these cabins more than a few times a day."

"No, not that. He opened the door and came out. He told me he never shuts the doors on cabins when he's working. That anyone walking down the passage-way could look in and see him. So why did he just come out of a closed cabin door?"

11

Olivia and Hayley walked down the crew hallway, their footsteps echoing off the metal walls
in the silence. They turned the corner and saw Alex's
office. They stopped, their hearts pounding.

Hayley took a step towards his office door, but
Olivia held her back. "My stomach is in knots."

Hayley shook her head. "Mine, too. But he needs
to know about the pictures. We can't keep evidence
away from him. What if he finds out later that we have
them?"

She started forward, but Olivia grabbed her arm.
"We need to think this through."

"What's going on?" Alex came out of his office. "Is
everything OK?"

"Yes... or, I don't know... I'm not sure... we found
something..." Her voice trailed off as she realized she
did not know how to explain this to him without him
getting mad.

"I found these photographs," Olivia said. "I think they might show the killer."

She handed Alex the envelope. He took it and opened it.

"I don't understand," Alex said. "These pictures were in the gallery?"

Olivia nodded. "Yes. I thought they were ours."

"But, they're not," Alex said.

"No," Olivia shook her head. "They're not."

She took a deep breath and let it out slowly. "They were in the file box behind the counter in the studio with all the crew photos in it. I thought they were the pictures he'd taken of Hayley and me, so I took them. But they weren't our pictures."

Alex shuffled through the photos. "Ok, they're just some modeling photos and pictures of him with his friends. Nothing here that seems out of order for a photographer to have. Why do you think they show the killer?"

Olivia explained Emilio's change in behavior after she mentioned Martin and his denial of being his friend, his fight with Anna, and Blake warning her to stay away from him.

Alex shook his head and rolled his eyes. "Nothing you have told me leads me to the conclusion that he murdered Martin. You can't go around accusing people of being murderers. People don't like that."

Olivia let out a frustrated breath. "We're not going around randomly accusing people. Hayley and I didn't say anything to anyone about our suspicions. We brought the evidence to you."

"Great. I'm glad you did, but nothing here is evidence of anything. Just some pictures."

"But why did Emilio lie about knowing Martin?"

"Maybe he wanted to get rid of the two of you and figured that saying he didn't know him would shut you up, so you'd leave."

"But, Emilio..."

"I need the two of you to stay out of the way."

Olivia put her hands on her hips and stomped her foot. "You aren't even trying,"

"I am trying," Alex said. "You do not know what I have been doing. I will not let you or Hayley impede my investigation."

"I'm sorry," Olivia said. "Emilio is the murderer. I'm going to prove it, even if it means that I have to do it myself."

Alex frowned. "You will not do anything concerning this case. I don't want you talking to anyone involved. No going to the photography studio, no questioning of Emilio, or anyone else for that matter. Do you understand?"

Olivia met his gaze and held it. Alex glared at her.

"Yes, I understand."

"Good."

"I understand, but I know I can help figure this out."

"I don't need your help. I can do this by myself." Alex's jaw clenched. "Get out of here. Both of you."

Hayley backed away.

Olivia lingered, looking at Alex. "I just want to help."

He stormed into his office, slamming the door behind him.

"Somehow that went even worse than I expected. He wouldn't even listen to me." Olivia shook her head.

"He's the security officer. We can't help if he won't listen to us. You just need to let it go."

"I can't. I'm going to find out where Emilio was when Martin was killed," Olivia said. "If he has an alibi, great, but I don't think he will. I think he murdered Martin. I'm going to prove it, even if it means that I have to do it myself."

Hayley shook her head. "No. You won't do anything. Alex was pretty clear he doesn't want us involved at all."

Olivia turned and glared at her. "How can you say that? Martin is dead. The killer is running free. What if he's someone we know? What if Alex goes after you, instead of tracking down Emilio? He didn't sound like he was even going to look at the possibility that Emilio might have done it. I have to do something."

"No. You don't. Leave it to Alex. He's a professional." Hayley yawned. "I'm worn out from doing my show and rehearsing for yours and we're going to have another late night tonight. Can I trust you to not get into any trouble trying to track down a killer while I take a nap?"

Olivia looked defiantly at Hayley and crossed her arms.

"Look, I totally appreciate you wanting to make sure I'm okay. But Alex is right. It is dangerous for you to go looking for a murderer. Promise me you'll leave this alone so I can go have a nap in peace."

Olivia could see the exhaustion on Hayley's face. "Okay, I'll behave myself so you can nap in peace."

Hayley swiped her key to her cabin and yawned again. "Do you want to go to the Midnight buffet before we rehearse tonight?"

"Sounds good. It's Tropical night, that's my favorite."

"I'll see you then." Hayley gently closed her door.

Olivia opened her cabin door and greeted Chico. She got him out of his cage and sat down on her bunk. Chico stepped down onto her knee. He fluffed up his neck feathers as Olivia rubbed his neck. "Ah, Chico, I should be rehearsing, but all I can think about is Emilio and if he killed Martin."

Chico rubbed his cheek against her finger, his eyes only half open. Olivia giggled as Chico purred like a cat. "Oh, my silly boy. What would I do without you?"

Chico lifted one leg and tucked his foot up into his breast feathers. He leaned against her hand as she rubbed his cheek. Olivia almost drifted off from rocking of the ocean and cuddling with Chico. She had too much to do to fall asleep. She sat up, startling Chico awake.

"I'm sorry, baby boy. I have to put you up and get moving so I can get the trunk ready for rehearsal with Hayley tonight. And I know I told Hayley that I would not look into Emilio anymore, but if I just happened to stop by and see Blake, Hayley can't be upset with me. Maybe when I see him, I'll ask him a little bit about what he knows about Emilio." Olivia put Chico in his cage.

"Bad Boy!"

"You're not a bad boy, Chico. I have to get some stuff done. Okay, buddy?"

"Oh, Pumpernickel!"

"Whatever you say, birdie boy."

Olivia changed Chico's food and water and headed up to the Purser's desk.

Sophie grinned ear to ear when she saw Olivia. She looked back at the door to Blake's office, but it was closed. "So, how was your hot date last night?"

Olivia rolled her eyes. "It wasn't a date."

Sophie laughed. "That's not the impression I got from Blake."

"Anyway... I have a question for you."

"Of course. What can I help you with?"

"The night Martin was killed. Did you see Emilio at all?"

Sophie thought for a second. "Gosh, it's hard to remember. It was so busy since it was the first night of the cruise and I had a huge line of passengers. I'm trying to think if I saw any of the casino staff that night. The cashier came by to pick up his drawer. Anna came by to make a payment on her bar account. I'm sorry. I can't remember if I saw Emilio or not. It was so busy. Why do you ask? Do you think he might be involved?"

The office door behind Sophie opened, and Blake walked out. His black hair was styled, his uniform crisp, but his grey eyes had dark circles under them. He made eye contact with Olivia, recognition washing over his face. "Hey! How are you feeling?"

"Better, thank you. How are you? You look tired."

Sophie picked up some papers from her desk area and walked over to the copy machine.

"Always exhausting joining a new ship."

"True."

"I was going to take a late lunch. Have you eaten?" Blake looked at Olivia expectantly.

"Actually, I haven't. My schedule is a mess today. I overslept."

"Then let's go grab some lunch. Sophie, I'll be back in a while. Radio me if you need me."

"Yes, sir." Sophie looked at Olivia and smiled at her. Going to lunch with Blake would fuel Sophie's assumption that they were dating.

She followed Blake to a quiet table in the back of the dining room. There were a few scattered tables of passengers eating. They ordered their meal, and Blake handed the menus to the waiter.

"I'm glad to see you looking better today. You had me worried last night."

"Thank you. I appreciate you getting me back to my cabin safely. Sorry about Chico. I guess he was grumpy that we woke him up." Olivia smiled. "He's a character."

"Yes, I could see that. So he lives in your cabin?"

Olivia's brow furrowed. "Of course. Where else would he live?"

"I don't know. Backstage, maybe? I guess I never really thought about it."

"Parrots are social animals. Chico would be miserable alone backstage."

Blake nodded. "That makes sense. It surprised me when he started talking to me."

"He's got a ton of personality. That's part of why I adopted him. He was so scared when I first met him, but he talked and sang to me. I knew if I could get him to trust me, he'd be a star in the show. And he is! Training him really bonded us."

"So, what are you up to today?" asked Blake.

"I should be rehearsing and working on some of my solo stuff for the show." Olivia sighed.

"Should be? Why aren't you? Other than having lunch with me."

"I just can't stop thinking about Martin. I'm worried that they won't catch the killer."

"Finding his killer isn't your responsibility."

"Alex, the safety officer, said the same thing. But he doesn't even seem to be investigating and trying to figure out who killed Martin." Olivia pushed her plate away. "I took him evidence and he just totally blew me off."

"Evidence?" Blake frowned and leaned in.

"Yes! I thought I had picked up an envelope of the photos that Martin had taken of Hayley and I, but there were a bunch of photos of Martin with his friends in them. One had him and Emilio, the Casino Manager. But, when I talked to Emilio, he denied being friends with Martin. I told Alex, but I don't think he was even going to talk to Emilio about it."

"Do you have these photographs?" Blake asked.

"No, I gave them to Alex."

"Other than Emilio, who else was in the pictures? Maybe there are other clues?"

"There were some modeling shots, but I didn't recognize anyone else."

"I think you need to leave this alone."

"You're not the first to tell me that." Olivia let out a long exhale. "I guess I need to put this aside for now and focus on getting ready for my show. I appreciate you talking this through with me."

Blake reached across the table and took Olivia's hand. "Of course, anytime. If you need to talk, I'm here to listen."

O livia stood in the center of the dark stage, only a ghost light lit behind her, casting dark shadows on her newspaper. The heavy velvet drapes were closed between her and the empty theatre. She held up her newspaper and tore it in two. She ripped the pile of paper until it was in small pieces. Olivia folded the pieces into a small bundle and then shook the newspaper loose.

A single square of newspaper floated to the floor as her hands separated, opening up her almost complete newspaper.

A sigh of frustration escaped her lips. She bent over and picked up the stray piece of paper. If this happened during the show, it would be over. She needed to get this trick right.

Olivia headed back to the dressing room and sat at the mirrored makeup table to reset the trick.

The light bulbs around the mirror evenly lit her face, showing off the dark circles under her bloodshot blue eyes.

This cruise was brutal, and she was exhausted. Peter dumping her, the responsibility of pulling off the show, and a murder all weighed on her.

She rested her chin on her hand and looked at her reflection. She only had a couple more days to get this show rehearsed and ready to perform in front of two thousand people. Why had she ever listened to Hayley? She couldn't do this. Why had she thought she could?

The show had always been Peter's. She was just "the girl" that he cut in half or floated up to the ceiling. Magic was his passion, not hers.

She put her head down on the table in front of her. Tears streamed out of her eyes, dripping on the white laminate. Her back heaved as she let the sobs she'd been holding back escape.

The scrape of the curtain on the track above the dressing room door startled her. She turned towards the door, tears still trailing down her cheeks.

A man in a white officer's uniform filled the doorway.

"Alex! You startled me."

"Sorry. I was doing my last rounds and saw a light on in here. I didn't think anyone would be in the dressing room this late. The shows have been over for hours. What are you doing here?" Alex pulled a handkerchief out of his pocket and handed it to her. "I didn't mean to, uh, interrupt."

Olivia wiped her smeared makeup off her cheeks. "I'm rehearsing for the show. Or I guess I should say, I am trying to rehearse. Can't seem to get anything to work right. I can't do this. I'm going to tell Tristan that I am going to sign off the ship when we get to Nassau. He needs to get another act to fly out and take over. Ugh. Sorry. Didn't mean to dump on you."

"What I've learned is that when someone cares enough about something to be upset about not doing as good a job as they want to, they usually are doing a superb job. Not many people would be up at this time of night working." Alex backed out the door. "I'll let you get back to uh.... rehearsing."

Alex pulled the curtain closed. Olivia watched the curtain fabric sway back and forth with the motion of the ship.

She turned back to her newspaper and finished re-setting it. She picked it up and walked back out on-stage. The light behind her reflecting off the white newsprint.

Olivia tore the newspaper in half, and then in half again, and finally in half one more time until it was a thick stack of squares of newspaper. She folded the stack in half, grabbed the corners, and pulled. The newspaper unfolded.

No pieces dropped to the floor.

She let out a breath she hadn't realized she'd been holding.

She walked over to her case and pulled out a set of large silver rings and began linking and un-linking them. She ended with a chain of 7 rings held high over her head, all linked to each other.

She put the rings back in their case and packed up for the night. She was getting too tired to concentrate. Olivia pushed all the cases into the dark recesses behind the stage. She walked through the dark theatre to the lobby.

The ship was quiet, only the casino and the disco still hopping.

Olivia pushed the down button on the elevator and watched the floors light up as the elevator made its way to her floor. The doors whooshed open, and she took a step in. A man was laying face down on the floor of the elevator.

She laughed to herself. Someone must have had a few too many cocktails in the disco and had passed out.

She squatted down and shook the man's shoulder. He didn't wake up. The elevator door tried to close on her. She stood up and pushed the open button. She tried to keep it pushed while she shook the man again. Finally, she grabbed his shoulder and turned him over.

Someone was screaming.

Olivia realized the person screaming was her.

E milio's tie was twisted tightly around his neck.
He was dead.

Olivia shoved the elevator door open and punched the emergency call button.

A voice came over the speaker. "Can I help you?"

"Yes, it's an emergency. Can you send security to these elevators?" Olivia's voice quavered.

"May I ask what the emergency is?" the disembodied voice asked.

"There is a dead man in the elevator. Please, call Alex. He's the security officer."

"I'll send someone right away."

Time slowed as she waited for Alex. Every creak and hum the ship made sent shivers up her spine.

Olivia held her breath as heavy footsteps quickly climbed the stairs. She kept her hand on the elevator door to keep it open and leaned to see who was coming up the stairs.

Alex's head rose above the stairs, his radio on his hip crackling.

"Olivia, what's going on?"

"It's Emilio. He's dead. I found him when the elevator door opened." Olivia moved out of the elevator.

Alex dropped to his knees and reached down to check for a pulse. He sat back on his heels, put his hands on his knees, and his head dropped.

Alex pulled his radio off his belt. He pushed a button on the side and a hiss of static erupted.

"Bridge."

"Sir, this is Safety Officer Ballas. I need assistance at the aft lift in front of the theatre."

"Stand by. I'll send back up."

Alex stood up and took out his keys. He inserted one into the panel of the elevator. The buzzing stopped, and the door stayed open without Olivia having to hold it. Her hands were shaking as she dropped them to her side. She backed away from the elevator and lowered herself onto a bench next to the lobby wall.

Alex walked over to her. "Tell me what happened."

"I really thought he'd killed Martin. Now he's dead. I should've...."

"Olivia, listen to me. This isn't your fault. And you shouldn't have done anything. Now, tell me what happened after I saw you."

"After you left, I rehearsed for a while longer and then packed up for the night. I pushed the down button on the elevator and when it opened, I thought a passenger had passed out drunk. I tried to wake him up and turn him over and that is when I realized it was Emilio." Tears spilled out of her eyes and she shook her head to clear the image from her mind.

Alex knelt down in front of her. "Did you see anything or hear anything or anyone?"

"No. I don't think so. Everything seemed normal until the elevator door opened and Emilio was laying there."

"Did you see anyone at all after I left the dressing room?"

"No, just you. The ship was quiet."

The noise of a group of people heading towards them got louder. Alex stood up. "They're almost here. Is there anything else I need to know?"

Olivia shook her head.

"Okay, I'm going to send one of my staff to escort you to your cabin."

Olivia jolted. "Do you think I killed him? Are you putting me under cabin arrest?"

"No, I want to make sure you get to your cabin safely. There is a murderer on this ship. You've been poking around and now you found a body. I don't want you to be next."

Olivia shivered.

"Stay here for now. Once I get my staff caught up, Victor will come get you, okay?"

Olivia nodded. She sat and watched as Alex briefed his staff. More officers arrived, adding to the noise and confusion in the lobby.

"Ma'am? Officer Ballas asked me to escort you to your cabin."

Victor walked her to her cabin and stood by as she fumbled with her key card to unlock her cabin door. Her hands were shaking.

"Thank you for making sure I got here safely."

"Of course. Officer Ballas wanted me to give you his card with his direct number."

Olivia took the card and shut the door. She put Alex's card in her wallet. Her cabin was quiet. Before she went up to rehearse, she'd put Chico to bed. Under his cage cover, she heard his sleepy sounds. She was glad he was sleeping. She was too worn out to deal with him right now.

She felt like she'd barely closed her eyes when her cabin phone rang.

"Did you hear what happened last night?" Haley asked.

"Last night?"

"Yes, Emilio was murdered. The entire ship is talking about it. I heard that someone found him in an elevator."

"Yeah, I know. I found him."

"What?!"

Olivia winced at Hayley's shriek. "I had been rehearsing. When I opened the elevator, he was there."

"No freaking way. Listen, I want to hear all about it. I'll be over in 5, okay?"

Before Olivia could answer, Hayley had hung up the phone.

"Good morning. Good, good morning." Chico grumbled in his gruff morning voice.

She looked at his cage and saw his eye peek out of the little hole in his cover. Olivia pulled off his cover. A frantic knocking startled them both.

"Good Gravy! Ah! Ah! Ah!" Chico flapped his wings frantically.

"Hang on Chico. It's ok. I think it is Hayley."

Chico sang his scales. "La, la la!"

Olivia walked up to her cabin door and put her hand on the knob to open it. She hesitated. She looked through the peephole. Hayley was standing shifting from foot to foot..

Olivia pulled the door open, and Hayley almost knocked her over on her way in.

"Girl, tell me everything."

"La, la la, Laaaa!"

"One minute, Chico. I'll pay attention to you in a minute. But first, I need to hear all about last night."

Olivia sighed and sat down on her bunk. She filled Hayley in on finding Emilio.

Hayley shook her head. "I can't believe this. I can't believe we have another murder on our ship. This is nuts. I don't want to sound like an awful person, but I'm so relieved I wasn't the last person someone saw with Emilio. When he was killed, I was sound asleep in my cabin. If Alex doesn't believe me, my roommate will vouch for me."

Olivia was relieved for her friend. It was awful having that hanging over her.

Olivia leaned back in her bed and hugged her legs to her chest. "So, who killed them both?"

Chico paced back and forth in his cage, his head bopping up and down. "Uh oh! Oh no!"

"Chico, settle down."

Hayley laughed and shook her head. "Chico is right. No thinking about who killed Martin and Emilio. You found a body last night. What if you had been a few minutes earlier and had found the killer? You would be dead. You need to stay away from this. I will not leave you alone until they find the killer."

"So you're going to babysit me until the killer is found? And I'm not allowed to figure out who that is?" Olivia crossed her arms. "Come on. I'm not planning to go after the killer myself, but if we can help figure out who had a motive to kill them both, we can take that to Alex and let him do his job and investigate."

"I'm sure Alex is perfectly capable of handling this all on his own."

"Is he though? He hasn't found the killer yet, and now another person is dead."

Haley's shoulder drooped.

Olivia sat up and leaned towards Hayley. "I don't want anyone else to die, do you?"

"Of course not." Hayley looked offended.

"I know you don't. I shouldn't have said it like that. If we can help find the murderer, we might prevent someone else from dying."

"So, what are you thinking?" Hayley got Chico out of his cage and pet his head, his neck feathers fluffed up.

Olivia got up and grabbed the notebook she'd bought for Peter. "Let's make a list of who we think might have known both Martin and Emilio."

"Alright, that sounds safe enough." Chico stood on one foot on Hayley's knee, his eyes dropping closed as she rubbed his cheeks.

Olivia clicked her pen open. "Well, number one on the list has to be Anna. We don't have proof that she was the woman who was fighting with Martin, but we know it wasn't you. We know they knew each other. She worked for Emilio. She kept looking at him when we were talking to her in the casino about the photographs. I thought it was because he was her boss and she didn't want to get in trouble for talking instead of working, but what if she was worried about him seeing us talking to her for another reason? Any ideas?"

"Could modeling be against her contract?" Hayley asked.

Olivia shook her head. "I doubt it. Plus, you don't strangle someone over a contract issue. I saw Anna and Emilio fighting when I was in the officer's mess, too."

"Other than Anna, and I guess me, who was a suspect in Martin's murder?"

"Alex was interviewing Joseph. Martin had yelled at him when his luggage cart almost knocked over Martin's tripod. Do you think Joseph knew Emilio?"

"Could Joseph be his room steward?" Hayley asked.

"I doubt it. Emilio would have a crew cabin, wouldn't he? Joseph only cleans entertainer and passenger cabins in this hall. I just can't see Joseph murdering anyone."

"Desperation will cause people to do horrible things. But I agree with you."

"At the same time, why was the door of the cabin closed when he told me he always leaves cabin doors open?"

Olivia wrote his name on her pad of paper. "I think our top suspect has to be Anna. Do you know anyone who knows Anna who might have some insight into her and Martin and Emilio?"

"She and Sophie are friends. Remember the day we all went to the beach? They hung out together all day."

Olivia nodded. "That make sense. She knew about Anna taking modeling pictures with Martin. Anna didn't seem to want anyone to know about that. Let's go ask Sophie what she knows."

"You said we were just going to make a list and try to talk things through."

"Talking to Sophie isn't dangerous. Plus, I won't be alone. You'll be with me."

Hayley smoothed out her sundress and smiled coyly at Olivia. "Could there be anyone else at the Purser's desk that you would want to see while we're there?"

"Oh goodness. I hadn't even thought about Blake."

Hayley laughed. "I'm sure you hadn't."

"Seriously, Hayley. I just got dumped. I am not ready to date anyone else. Blake seems nice. I guess I'm not there yet."

"He's dreamy."

"I'm not saying he's not handsome. I'm just not sure I'm ready to date."

Hayley picked Chico up and gave him a kiss on the top of his head. "At least you have this handsome fella keeping you company."

"Very true."

"Mwah! Kiss, kiss, kiss." Chico made kissing noises as Hayley put him on his perch.

14

"**M**ate! I heard you found the bloke in the lift." Sophie leaned in, waiting to hear what had happened.

Olivia grimaced. She dreaded everyone on the ship knowing she'd found Emilio. "Yes, it is true. I found him."

"Ah, bless! I was going to come check on you, but I've been going flat out all morning."

"I'm alright, but thank you for worrying about me."

"Of course I was worried about you. I'm worried about Anna, too. This devastated her." Sophie shook her head.

"Anna?"

"You know she and Emilio were engaged? I took some brekky to her cabin this morning when I first heard about him."

Olivia looked at Sophie. Her eyes widened. "I had no idea."

"Well, it wasn't common knowledge. I knew, of course. They were trying to keep it hush-hush since he was her boss. Let's keep it between us?" Sophie looked at them both questioningly.

"Of course. We won't say anything."

Olivia looked towards the office door. Sophie followed her gaze. "Looking for the new boss man, are you?"

"No, I just..."

"Well, you can look, but you won't find him. He went back to his cabin. He fell in the shower and bumped that pretty face of his. When I saw what a mess he was, I told him I could handle it today and to go to the doc and have a lie in."

"That's awful. Poor guy."

Sophie picked up a stack of papers. "I was just about to head to his cabin and take these to him to sign, but I want to check on Anna. Could you run them by his cabin for me?"

"Sophie, I don't need an excuse to go see Blake."

"I'm not setting you up. It would really help me out. I'll be late for my lunch if I have to go up all the way to the officer's quarters before I go all the way down to the crew deck to check on Anna. I need to eat lunch at some point, too."

Olivia took the papers from Sophie and looked at Hayley. "Shall we?"

"Wouldn't you rather go by yourself?"

"No, actually I wouldn't. Aren't you the one that was worried about me walking around the ship alone?"

"True, okay, I'll come with you. You realize you are taking a risk that he'll fall madly in love with me?"

"I'm completely happy to take that risk. Who doesn't fall madly in love with you?"

"Now you're talking." Hayley put her arm around Olivia's shoulder. "Let's go."

Their footsteps were the only sound in the officer's corridor. Most of the officers were either working long days or sleeping from their long night's work. Olivia gently knocked on Blake's door.

"Who is it?"

"Blake, it's me, Olivia."

They could hear shuffling in the cabin. The door opened partway. The cabin was dark behind him and he stood in the half shadow of the door.

"Sophie asked us to bring these to you. She needs you to sign them for her."

Blake took the papers and went to his small desk. He pulled out a pen, signed them, and handed them back to Olivia. "Thanks."

He started to shut the door. Olivia put her hand on the door and held it open. "Are you okay?"

"Yep."

"Good. See you later."

Blake shut the door.

Olivia looked at Hayley. "That was weird."

"He's probably embarrassed that he fell down. Doesn't want to show weakness to you."

"I guess. Or he's not as into me as you and Sophie thought."

"Highly doubtful. You are gorgeous, smart, and talented. How could he not be into you?"

"Hayley, I wasn't fishing for compliments. I am not in a place to date. I need to get my act together, both literally and figuratively."

Hayley hung her head. "With finding out about Emilio, I totally forgot to ask you how your rehearsal went last night."

"It was kind of a disaster at first. I have my parts of the show that I've been doing for years and I know I can do them. But, now I have to do Peter's parts too and it's overwhelming. I gotta be honest. I had a meltdown in the dressing room and had a good cry."

Hayley hugged Olivia. "Ah, babe. I'm sorry. I wish I could give Peter a piece of my mind for hurting you. That swine."

"You're already helping me so much by being my friend and doing the show with me. I don't know what I would do otherwise."

"Glad to help. I'm excited about it. So, after your good cry, did you feel better?"

"Actually, I felt pretty embarrassed. Alex found me sobbing in the dressing room when he did his last rounds."

Hayley laughed. "He doesn't seem like the type of guy who would handle a crying woman very well."

"I'm sure he was uncomfortable, but he was caring and encouraging. He actually helped me. After he left, I went out on stage and made some actual progress on my torn and restored newspaper and linking rings."

"Oh Livy, that is awesome. I'm so happy for you! See, I knew you could do it."

"Well, I haven't done it yet. We still have so much left to do before the show."

Hayley nodded. "I know. I have a couple of nights off now, so I'll be able to put more time into rehearsing."

Sophie was back at the purser's desk when they got there. Some of her curly black hair had escaped her ponytail and her cheeks were flushed. "Hey girls. What a freakin' day. Anna wasn't in her cabin and by the time I got to the mess, I'd missed lunch. Didn't have time to run to the buffet before my break was over since we're short staffed. Did Blake sign the papers?"

Olivia handed the stack of papers to Sophie. "He did. Do you want us to go grab you something to eat off the buffet?"

"Probably won't hurt me to miss a meal. Ship life hasn't been all that friendly to my figure. Too much good food." Sophie pulled out an orange. "I have some fruit. I'll snack on that. But thank you for the offer."

A couple walked up to the desk, needing help from Sophie. Hayley and Olivia waved at Sophie and let her get back to work.

"Do you want to go to afternoon tea? I think I need a snack to make up for not sleeping much last night."

Hayley pushed the button for the Lido deck. "Sounds good to me."

Olivia picked out a tart with a butter cookie crust, custard and fruit. Hayley picked out some cookies. They brought their hot tea and treats over to a table by the window.

Hayley let out a sigh. "I think I'm going to adopt having afternoon tea when I get off of ships. Such a brilliant addition to the day."

"Agreed." Olivia took a bite. "So good. Enough sugar to fuel me for a few hours."

"What are we going to work on tonight?" Hayley asked.

"I was thinking we'd haul out the..." Olivia stopped talking. She looked past Hayley.

Hayley turned around and saw Anna sitting at a table with other casino staff.

"I guess that's why Sophie couldn't find her in her cabin. She doesn't seem too devastated, does she?" Olivia shook her head. "Your fiancé is murdered and you go to afternoon tea."

"According to Sophie, Anna didn't want anyone to know that she and Emilio were engaged. Maybe she's still trying to keep their relationship quiet."

Olivia leaned in towards Hayley and lowered her voice. "Or maybe she killed him and Martin. I wonder where she was last night when Emilio was killed."

Anna got up and walked up to the buffet.

"I'll be right back. I'm going to go ask her some questions."

Hayley stood up and blocked Olivia. "No, you're not. If she killed them, the last thing you need to do is to confront her."

Olivia sunk back down into her chair and let out a frustrated sigh. "You sound like Alex."

"I don't want you getting hurt. Alex doesn't either."

"Fine. I need to grab some veggies for Chico. I'm sure he's ready for his afternoon tea, too."

"That bird eats more than most humans."

"He's very food motivated. But that is part of what makes him so easy to teach things to. He'll learn anything for a good snack."

"Ha! Same. Maybe you need to bring snacks to get me to learn the tricks for the show!"

Olivia laughed. "I'll see what I can do."

As they walked out of the buffet, Olivia shivered as she saw Anna looking at her with a stony stare. 'Something is off with her."

"Not your problem, Olivia."

"Fine. Let's meet up backstage after the second show is over."

"Works for me."

Olivia could hear Chico talking before she got to her cabin. "Mmm mmm! Treat!" Her cabin door was open.

Joseph almost bumped into her coming out of her cabin. "Excuse me. Sorry. I turned your bed down already. I hope that's alright."

"Sure, that's fine."

Joseph's face was flushed and sweaty. He wasn't looking at her, but at his cart down the passageway. "Do you need more towels or anything?"

"No, Joseph. I don't need anything. Are you okay?"

"Yes, ma'am."

As he walked away, she saw Joseph put something in his jacket pocket.

Olivia looked around her cabin. She didn't see anything missing.

"What are you doing?" Chico asked.

"Oh, you want your veggies, I'm guessing?"

"Zipadee!"

Olivia handed him a carrot and put the extra vegetables she'd gotten for him in his dish.

Joseph was acting very strangely.

H ayley pumped her arms like a bodybuilder. "Other than the levitation, I think that went pretty darn good, if I do say so myself. The levitation is so frustrating for me. I'm sorry I keep messing that up. I get so nervous."

"Being nervous is what is messing you up. You need to relax. When you get nervous and start stressing, you wiggle, and that gets you off balance. The entire trick rocks and sways. You need to let go and breathe into it." Olivia took a deep breath and motioned for Hayley to take one with her.

"I totally get what you're saying. Unfortunately, my feet don't seem to understand and freak out when they realize they are 6 feet off the ground."

Olivia laughed. "Maybe we need to get them closed toed shoes so they can't see the ground."

Hayley smiled and shook her head. "So I have an idea for tomorrow when we get to Nassau. Do you want to go to the zoo with me?"

Olivia's face fell. "Oh no! I really want to go. That had been my plan before Peter ditched. I really shouldn't, though. When the ship is quiet, I need to use that time to rehearse my solo parts of the show."

"Oh, come with me. You are doing great. We'll rehearse again tomorrow night."

Olivia crossed her arms. "I can't. I need to rehearse my solo stuff tomorrow afternoon and then we can go over our stuff tomorrow night."

Hayley sighed. "You said you had a great run through last night. You can't miss your chance to see flamingos."

"I know. You can't imagine how much I want to see the flamingos. But I'm so nervous that I will mess up the show."

Hayley looked around the stage. "How about this? You do a run-through of the torn and restored newspaper and the linking rings and if you get them both right, you come with me. If you drop a ring or your paper has holes in it, you stay here."

Olivia laughed. "So, you know my two night-mares?"

Hayley picked up the black velvet bag with the linking rings and shoved it at Olivia. "Show me what you've got, girl."

Olivia took the bag, opened it up, and pulled out the rings.

She shook her head. "I'm not ready. If I had a month, maybe I could pull this off. I'm so scared that I am going to bomb. I'll get kicked off the ship, and then what will I do? There aren't many people out there wanting to hire a magician's assistant. I don't even know where I would go or what I would do if I got kicked off the ship."

"Then we'll make sure you don't get kicked off. I know you can do this. Remember what you told me just a few minutes ago? You need to let go and breathe into it."

Olivia chuckled. "Boy, you don't play fair. Throwing my own words right back at me!"

Hayley grinned at her. "Deep breath in.... and out. Now go link those rings, baby!"

Olivia pushed play on her music and walked to the center stage, directly under the stage light. Her music cue came on and she began her routine.

Hayley sat cross-legged on the edge of the stage and watched Olivia.

Olivia's routine was almost a dance with the rings as her partner instead of a magic trick. She linked and unlinked the rings while gracefully moving across the stage. She ended with all the rings linked above her head, stretching from hand to hand.

"Oh, Olivia. That was..."

"I know it isn't funny like what Peter always did. I watched recordings and tried to memorize what he said and do it just like he did, but I couldn't get it to work. Why did I think I could do this? I'm not a magician. It was awful, wasn't it?" Hayley rubbed her temples.

"No!" Haley grabbed Olivia's shoulders and looked her in the eye. "Listen to me, Sis. That was so beautiful. I've never seen anything like that and I have seen a lot of different magic acts since I got on ships. I think it was so good because you aren't a magician. You didn't do the same cheesy routine every other magician does. I really loved it."

"Really?"

"Really. You looked like a ballerina with enchanted rings."

Olivia's face lit up and her cheeks flushed.

Hayley grinned. "You know what the best part is?"

"What?"

"Now you have to come to the zoo with me."

Olivia laughed. "I guess I do."

Olivia was changing the papers in Chico's cage when Hayley banged on her door.

"Ready for some fancy flamingos?"

"I'm a good boy!" Chico bobbed back and forth.

Hayley walked over and pet his cheek through the cage bars. "You are a good boy, and the only bird for us. I promise."

Chico made a kiss sound, and Hayley and Olivia made them back to him as they left Olivia's cabin.

They dashed down the flights of stairs to the gangway. Passengers crowded the dock, heading off to tours or the beach. Hayley and Olivia dodged people until they got out to the road. They headed to the taxi stand and grabbed a taxi to the zoo.

Two blue and gold macaws greeted them from their perch as they entered the grounds. Hayley sang to them, but they just looked at her.

"Don't feel bad. Macaws aren't known for their singing ability. Not like parrots, like Chico."

Hayley and Olivia visited the turtles and the peacocks. One peacock lifted his tail and shook his tail feathers at them. "Is he showing off or threatening us?"

"Maybe a little of both. Aren't you impressed with his plumage; but also a little nervous about going closer?"

"True. He nailed it." The peacock shook his tail towards them again, and Hayley jumped back.

"He will not get you. Peacocks are pretty peaceful birds."

Hayley and Olivia saw the palm-thatched roof around the flamingo area and sped up to get there before the performance started. They stood behind the fence and waited for the flamingos to enter. She loved all birds, but flamingos were one of her favorites. Next to Chico, of course.

A small gate opened, and a dozen or so pink flamingos ran out onto the grass, honking. Their trainer followed them around the circle.

One flamingo fell behind and the trainer walked towards the bird. The flamingo flapped, exposing a black stripe of feathers under his wings as he caught up to the other birds. The trainer called out commands, and the flamingos went from place to place in a group. They came right up to the fence in front of them. The flamingo closest to them stood on one foot and stretched his wing straight out to the side. The trainer shouted another command and the flamingos moved to another section.

When the show was over, Hayley looked at Olivia. "A little different from a trained parrot, but they were so cute."

"Agreed. I remember the first time I saw a flamingo in person. They almost didn't look real."

The man standing next to them looked worn out. His three kids were each going in a different direction. He said to his wife. "Man, I wish the flamingo's trainer would train the kids."

The girls giggled as they walked toward the monkeys.

A small monkey put his hands together and gave Olivia a pleading look like he was hoping she'd give him a treat.

"He must smell Chico's treats on you."

Olivia rolled her eyes. "He probably knows that I'm an easy mark for any cute critter. Gosh, do you think we could add a monkey to the show?"

"Are you going to sneak him out of here?"

"I wish. He's so cute! Oh! Let's go in with the lorikeets."

A lorikeet flew up onto Olivia's head. Hayley quickly snapped her picture. The lorikeet danced back and forth on her head and slid down her hair. Olivia laughed as she swayed back and forth with the lorikeet riding her hair like a swing.

Hayley giggled at the bird using Olivia as a playground. "At every exhibit, the animals go right towards you. I guess they can tell you are an animal person."

"I truly don't understand people who don't like animals. How could you not love something this adorable?"

The lorikeet flapped its wings to climb back up on Olivia's head.

"Ouch!" Olivia covered her eye with her hand. "His wing got me in the eye."

Hayley shooed the bird off of her head.

"No! It isn't his fault. He didn't mean it." The lorikeet flew off of her head and landed on another zoo visitor's shoulder.

Tears ran down Olivia's cheek. She put her hand over her eye. "Oh gosh. Just what I need."

Olivia took her hand off her eye, but the light made her blink and tear up again. "Do you think I can do the show with one hand over my eye? This really stinks."

Hayley looked at her eye but couldn't see anything in it. "His wing probably scratched your cornea. We need to get you back to the ship and see the doctor. We need to make sure it's not serious."

A zoo staff member stood in the pathway holding an enormous snake. The snake wound around her waist and arm. Hayley shivered. The staff member invited people to come up and pet the snake. Hayley stepped back and stepped on a man's foot behind her. "Oh, I'm so sorry."

"Don't worry. You didn't hurt me." He looked at Olivia, her eye blinking from the sun. "Are you flirting?"

Olivia put her hand back over her eye and focused on the man standing behind her and Hayley. "Alex?"

"Sure is."

"Oh, I almost didn't recognize you in your street clothes."

Alex looked down at his shorts and t-shirt. "I don't wear my uniform off the ship."

"Of course. Sorry about the blinking. I hurt my eye and can't stop it."

Olivia kept her hand over her eye. "Are you enjoying the zoo?"

"Probably more than you are. What happened to your eye?"

"A lorikeet flapped his wing and scratched my eye."

"Ah, I guess I'm glad a bird attacked you instead of by someone who didn't want to be interviewed like they were a suspect in a murder."

"I didn't get attacked by a bird. He was trying to get back on top of my head and accidentally brushed my eye with his wing."

"I wasn't trying to defame the bird. I like animals." Alex smiled.

"You do?" Olivia cocked her head.

"Yeah, I grew up on a farm. We always had a lot of animals," Alex said.

"And I didn't interview anyone." Olivia shrugged. "I just asked a couple of questions."

"Generally, people don't like to be asked questions about a murder. That's why it is my job."

"Yes, you have made that very clear." Olivia took Hayley's elbow. "We're actually headed back to the ship. I'm going to get the doctor to take a look at it."

"Good idea. Want to share a cab?"

"Oh, you should stay and enjoy the rest of the zoo."

"I'm back on duty in an hour. I was going to leave in a minute, anyway."

Olivia looked at Hayley to see if she would come up with a reason why they couldn't share a cab, but Hayley shrugged.

They made their way out to the taxi stand. Alex hailed a taxi and negotiated the rate back to the ship.

They climbed in the back of the taxi, Olivia in the middle between Alex and Hayley. The taxi driver drove like he was in a race to get them back to the ship.

Olivia tried to brace herself from falling on Hayley or Alex as they went around turns. She took her hand off her eye to maintain her balance, but her eye watered again.

She covered her eye as they went around a corner. The force of the turn flung her into Alex. He held her upright with his shoulder. She looked at him and her eye winked.

He laughed.

She covered her hurt eye and glared at him with her other eye.

The taxi pulled up in front of the dock.

Alex got out of the taxi and reached down to help Olivia.

She ignored his hand and got out by herself.

They flashed their IDs to the officer on the gangway.

"Good luck at the doctor." Alex headed towards his cabin. "I hope your eye will be alright."

"Thank you. I'm sure it will be. How much damage can a feather do?"

16

Olivia leaned her elbow on the metal arm of her chair in the small mint green waiting room of the infirmary, her hand shielding her eye from the glare of the harsh neon light.

The doctor opened the door and walked out into the waiting room. "So, what do we have here?"

"Hi Dr. Kohli. I hurt my eye and was hoping you could check it out for me."

"Of course, Olivia. What happened this time?"

"A rainbow lorikeet accidentally hit me in the eye with his wing."

"Ah, like the squirrel you were feeding accidentally nipped your finger last month?"

Olivia shrugged and looked down. "Not exactly like that."

Hayley jumped in. "She was at the zoo in the enclosure with the lorikeets. One brushed her eye with his wing."

"Well, let's take a look and see what we have." Dr. Kohli pulled down a fresh swath of paper and patted the examination table. "Hop on up."

Olivia lifted herself onto the table and laid down. Dr. Kohli turned on the bright overhead light, moved the magnifier over her face, and looked into her eye. The bright light made Olivia's eye blink and water. Dr. Kohli held her eye open as he looked closer.

"Looks like you have a scratched cornea. Not very serious."

Olivia sat up and breathed out in relief. "Good news."

Dr. Kohli opened a drawer in a green metal cabinet and pulled out an eye patch. "Wear this for 24 hours and you should be fine. I'll give you some drops to help with the pain."

"An eye patch?" Olivia's shoulders drooped.

"Need to protect it so it can heal."

"Ugh. This is awful." Olivia slumped down on the exam table. "I have a show in a couple of days."

Dr. Kohli walked Hayley and Olivia back out into the waiting room and handed Olivia a small bottle of eye drops. "All the more reason to follow my instructions and wear the eye patch."

Olivia crossed her arms.

"Now, now Olivia."

"What an awful week." Tears rolled down Olivia's cheeks. "I don't know how much more I can deal with."

Dr. Kohli put his hand on her chin and lifted her face so she was looking him in the eye. "It could be worse."

"Oh, really?" Olivia's brow furrowed in frustration.

"Yes, really."

"You mean Blake falling in the shower and hitting his head?" Olivia asked.

"Blake?"

"The purser."

"Ah! Blake. I didn't know he was on board. But no, I didn't mean him."

Dr. Kohli put his hand on her shoulder.

"You came in with a minor abrasion on your cornea. I have two crew members in the morgue behind you, who would have much preferred your week."

Olivia glanced at the unmarked door Dr. Kohli had gestured to and took a step away.

"Oh, Dr. Kohli. I'm sorry. I didn't mean to whine." She opened the eye patch and put it on. "You are right.

I should be grateful that this is all that is wrong with me."

"It's been a rough week on the Starlight. We're all feeling a little overwhelmed." Dr. Kohli put his hand on Olivia's shoulder. "I heard you found Emilio."

"Yes. I did. It was pretty awful."

"A traumatic experience for you."

"I'm sorry I overreacted to the eye patch."

"Sometimes it is the little things that put us over the edge when we have a lot of big stressors in our lives. I am going to prescribe some rest, relaxation, and some sunshine."

Hayley stepped forward. "I'll make sure she follows your prescription."

"And Hayley, make sure she behaves herself and doesn't 'accidentally' wrestle any alligators or feed a bear, okay?"

Hayley laughed. "Yes, sir. I'll do my best."

The door to the infirmary swung shut behind them.

"I do not know how Dr. Kohli can stand being below deck, in that dark office, with the morgue right behind him." Olivia shivered.

They climbed up the grey metal staircases until they reached the passenger area.

"Thank goodness I haven't done the show yet and none of the passengers recognize me. I feel so ridiculous with this stupid eye patch."

"It's not that bad. Want to get into our bathing suits and get some rest, relaxation, and sun like Dr. Kohli prescribed?"

"Just what I need, an eye patch shaped tan line around one eye."

"You can lie on your stomach. The sun will do you a world of good. A couple of frozen cocktails won't hurt either. Most of the passengers are still on shore, so the pool will be quiet."

"A frozen cocktail sounds pretty wonderful. I'll get into my swimsuit. Come get me when you're ready to head up."

Olivia opened her cabin door, and Chico squeaked and fell off his perch. He backed into the corner of his cage.

"Chico, you silly chicken bird." Olivia took her eye patch off. "It's me. See?"

She put the drops in her eye and put the patch back on.

Chico looked at her warily but didn't fall off his perch this time. Olivia put on her bikini and tied her batik sarong around her waist.

She got Chico out of his cage. He ran up her arm and sat on her shoulder. Olivia shook her head. "You know you aren't supposed to sit on my shoulder."

She tried to get him to step onto her hand, but a knock at her door sidetracked her. "That must be Haley."

Olivia opened the door.

Alex looking amused. "Ahoy matey!"

Olivia realized how ridiculous she looked in her bikini, with an eye patch, and a parrot on her shoulder.

Chico didn't help matters when he shouted, "Argh!"

"Alright, Chico, back in your cage."

"He's fine. You don't need to put him away on my account. I stopped by to check on you and see what Dr. Kohli had to say about your eye."

"Well, as you can see, he wants me to wear this eye patch, and he gave me some drops. I just put them in and I think they are helping."

"Good, glad to hear that. Bye, Chico."

"Goodbye! See ya later! Bye-bye! Adios!" Chico danced back and forth on Olivia's shoulder.

Alex laughed. "He's a real character."

"That he is."

"If you need anything, let me know."

"Thanks."

Olivia was about to shut the door when Hayley turned the corner. "Are you ready for the pool?"

"Yeah, just let me put Chico up."

"It was nice of Alex to check on you."

"Yeah, I guess so."

"Elevator or stairs."

"Stairs."

Hayley and Olivia ran up the first couple flights of stairs. They slowed the higher they climbed. They were out of breath by the time they reached the pool deck.

"Well, that was a workout." Hayley put her hand on her waist, pushing on the stitch in her side.

"I guess we worked off a cocktail or two climbing those stairs." Olivia panted, trying to catch her breath.

They found two lounge chairs towards the back of the pool deck in a quiet area.

Olivia grabbed towels from the bin and laid them out on their lounge chairs.

Hayley went up to the bar and ordered two drinks. She handed one to Olivia.

Olivia took a sip of the frozen cocktail. "Mmm, coconut rum. Excellent choice."

Hayley sat down on her lounge chair and took a long sip of her drink. She put the cup down. She sighed and picked it back up and took another sip. "Look Honey. I have something I have been dreading telling you, but you deserve to know."

Olivia sat up and swung her legs off of the lounge chair onto the deck so she faced Hayley. "What is it? Are you not going to do the show with me?"

"No, no, not that."

"Oh, thank goodness. I'd have to pack up my bags, grab Chico, and walk off the ship if you couldn't do the show with me."

"I promised to do the show."

"I know you did, but you are having such a hard time with the levitation. I thought you might have decided that you wouldn't do it."

"The levitation terrifies me. But that isn't anywhere near as scary as having to tell you this." Hayley looked down at the deck under her feet.

Olivia sat back. "What is it?"

"It's about Peter."

"Did you talk to him?"

"No." Haley shook her head. "Do you remember the dancer in the revue show named Candi?"

"The one with the red hair?"

"Yes, her. Her contract ended last cruise. That is why the cast had the extra rehearsal this week. We needed to train the new dancer." Hayley shifted in her seat. "Peter left with Candi."

Olivia pulled the eye patch off her eye and dropped it in her lap. She leaned forward and put her head in her hands. Her blonde hair fell, covering her face.

Hayley stood up and sat next to Olivia on the lounge chair. She tucked Olivia's hair behind her ear and rubbed her back. "The cast was talking in the dressing room after the show. Apparently, Candi and Peter got booked on another ship doing their own variety show. She is going to sing and dance and he is doing magic."

"So this wasn't a spur-of-the-moment thing? They've been planning this." Olivia wiped tears off her cheeks. "I hate that I cry when I am angry."

"I know."

"When I read his letter, I thought he was just needed a break. He didn't say anything about there being anyone else or doing another show. I don't even know what to say."

"If it makes you feel any better, the stage manager said that Peter tried to take off the magic illusions, but the officer wouldn't let him because he hadn't filled out the paperwork to get it off the manifest."

Olivia let out a tight laugh. "Ha! I always do the paperwork. He probably didn't even know that it needed to be done, since he always leaves that stuff for me to do. So, he's going to do a magic show on a ship with none of his props?"

"That is what it sounded like. He had a meltdown at the dock when he was trying to sign off the ship. They called security on him and told him if he didn't leave the dock immediately, they were going to call the port police."

"Wow. So all the cast knows this? This is so embarrassing." Olivia rubbed her forehead and covered her hurt eye with her hand to protect it from the sun.

"The stage manager was called down to the gangway to bring the illusion cases backstage after Peter left."

"That explains why all the cases were in a different order than how I had put them back. Oh, no! Do you think Tristan knows? He's going to be livid that I haven't talked to him."

Olivia stood up, but Hayley pulled her back down to the lounge chair. "Sweetie, are you going to go tell him in your bikini?"

"Of course not. I'll need to change first."

"Let's do one more run through tonight and then tell him. That way, we can give him an honest assessment of where we are with the show and if we can actually pull it off. It'll be fine. I promise."

"It's a disaster."

Olivia picked up her eye patch and put it back on her eye. She looked out at the horizon line to focus her vision.

A woman in a white blouse and black miniskirt walked in front of her, blocking her view. She reached in the pocket of her skirt and brought out a piece of paper. She looked at the paper, tore it up, and threw it overboard.

The woman turned and walked back towards the pool.

Olivia elbowed Hayley. "Look. It's Anna. Did you see that? She just tore up something and threw it overboard."

Olivia got up, ran to the rail, and looked overboard, but couldn't see the pieces of paper.

O livia tried to keep the exasperation out of her voice. "Hayley, you need to relax. You are shaking so much that the entire trick is rocking back and forth."

"I know, but I can't. As soon as you lifted me up, I got scared again. I'm so mad at myself! I don't know what to do. Maybe I just can't do this trick."

"Don't be mad at yourself. You are doing the best you can."

"I'm so sorry. I do not want to let you down, but I can't stop shaking. The waves keep rocking me back and forth. The levitation swaying freaks me out when I'm up there."

"I guess it is harder on sea than on land to do some tricks. I never really thought about it."

"How on earth did you do this trick when the sea was rough? The ocean is pretty calm right now, but I still feel like I'm going to fall."

"This is going to sound nuts, but I think I imagined that I was really flying. That I was weightless. When the ship would hit a wave, I'd just ride it out."

Hayley shrugged. "I don't know if I have a good enough imagination for that. I don't forget for even a second that I'm hooked up to all that stuff and swinging above the stage floor."

Olivia backed up to the closed stage curtain. They'd left it closed so that no one would come into the theatre and accidentally see how the trick worked. She looked up at the rigging above the stage, trying to figure out a solution. She closed her eyes and went through the show to see if there was any other trick she could move to the finale and still have enough time to fill the show.

"We need the 4 minutes this illusion takes. I don't have enough tricks that I know how to do to fill in the time. Some of the stuff Peter did, I don't know how to do and I don't have the time to learn them. The sleight of hand is beyond me right now. This illusion is the finale of the show. I don't have time to figure out anything else."

"Are you sure we can't switch parts?"

"I thought about that, but I'm wearing Chico in my costume. We don't have time to train you to steal Chico and teach him to fly from you up to me."

"I could do it. I'm sure I could."

"Chico's used to this trick because it is what Peter and I did at the end of the opening. But we don't know what he'd do if you tried to do it. "

"Chico loves me. I'm sure we could do it."

"Chico loves you. But he loves me too, and it took us weeks to get this trick right."

Hayley sighed. "I shouldn't have asked you, anyway. I am the one that said I would do this, so I need to figure it out."

Hayley looked at the levitation and nodded her head. "I will figure it out."

"No, you have worked so hard to help me. I shouldn't have ever put you in this position. I should have gone to Tristan and told him that Peter was gone and signed off the ship as soon as I could." Olivia's voice quavered. "The very least Peter could have done is tell me, so I could have signed off, too. I am so freaking angry at Peter for putting me in this place."

Olivia sat down on top of the levitation's case and put her head in her hands.

Hayley sat next to her.

"I don't even have a home to go to. We've been on ships so much for the last ten years, it didn't make any sense to pay for a house when we'd never be there. I haven't had a normal job in years. I keep telling myself I need to just get through this show and then I can look at what my future holds, but I'm feeling so defeated."

Hayley rubbed Olivia's back and put her arm around her shoulders. "You will not have to get off the ship. We'll figure this out."

Olivia put her head on Hayley's shoulder. "I hope so."

The stage curtain swayed back and forth and the ship crested a wave. Olivia saw someone tug at the curtain, trying to find the opening. She looked at Hayley and put her finger to her lips to signal her to stay quiet.

They stood up and slipped behind the illusion case.

A hand came through the overlap of the curtains.

Olivia and Hayley took another step back into the darkness of the backstage area.

The hand pulled the curtain back.

"Olivia?"

"Blake? What are you doing back here this late?"
Olivia walked into the light of the stage.

"What happened to your eye?" Blake asked.

"Nothing. Just a silly accident with a bird wing. Dr. Kohli said I can take the eye patch off tomorrow."

"That's good."

Hayley walked up next to her.

Blake took a step back. "Oh Hayley. You're here too, didn't see you there. I came to say sorry for being short with you earlier when you came to my cabin. I was not myself."

"It's fine. I hope you are alright?"

"Yep. I hope your eye feels better soon." Blake pushed through the overlapping curtains and left.

"Nice of him to come apologize," Hayley said.

"Yeah. I guess. I hadn't given him one more thought honestly."

"Sure you didn't." Hayley laughed.

Olivia gave Hayley a dirty look and rolled her eyes.

Hayley walked back to the levitation. "I can't do anything about Peter or Alex or the murderer, but by golly, I am going to make this show work. Look, I am going to stay here a little while longer. I'll get on the levitation trick and lay on it with it low to the ground.

If I can do it at two feet or four feet off the ground, then I will figure out how to do it 8 or 10 feet high."

Olivia felt a glimmer of hope. "You know, that might actually work. Should we run the trick a couple of times, but lower?"

"It really doesn't change anything for you. How about I stay and run it myself a few times? You go feed Chico and get to sleep. You have been up late every night this cruise and I know how worn out you are."

Olivia shook her head. "I'm exhausted, but I can't leave you here alone."

Hayley walked Olivia to the red velvet curtains. "Seriously, I can do this on my own. In fact, it'll be better for me to be alone. I can concentrate on relaxing with no distractions."

"Are you sure?"

"I am totally sure. Now git. Go get some rest." Hayley pulled the curtain back and waved Olivia out.

"But, shouldn't..."

"Girl, I said go feed Chico before he wastes away to nothing."

"It would take more than one late meal for that to happen." Olivia hugged Hayley. "Thank you. Chico will thank you for the late-night snack."

The curtain whooshed closed behind her. Olivia carefully walked up the rake of the aisle through the dark rows of seats.

The lobby was empty. She decided to take a minute on her way to her cabin and go look at the stars, since this might be her last opportunity before getting kicked off the ship. Chico had two full dishes of food. He'd be fine for a few minutes.

She threaded her way through the crew area to the crew deck below the Bridge where it was completely dark. It was the best place on the ship to watch the stars. Olivia breathed in the salty air. The whooshing wind blew her hair straight out behind her and hummed in her ears.

Olivia walked across the dark deck to the bow of the ship. She turned and looked up at the Bridge a couple of stories above her. It was dark, but she knew that there were officers up there. Even with auto-pilot, a living, breathing officer needed to be on the Bridge at all times. She wondered if they could see her down here in the dark.

The ship was cruising slowly through the water.

They didn't have far to go to get to the private island tomorrow. The ship didn't need to rush to their next destination.

The crests of the waves glistened like diamonds in the moonlight. The breeze felt so good. Olivia relaxed, listening to the splash of the waves against the hull of the ship. She loved this peaceful part of the ship.

Olivia hadn't cared about working on ships in the beginning. She just wanted to be with Peter. It was Peter's dream to be a magician, not hers.

Now, the idea of going back on land and not getting to experience the beauty of life on board a ship, day in and day out, felt like it would be such a blow.

Olivia knew she was fortunate to have gotten to live this life for the past ten years. She should be fine with starting over on land, but losing experiences like standing on this deck, looking at the crescent moon over the ocean, hit her like a gut punch.

She realized she had fallen in love with this lifestyle.

She needed to perform her show in front of two thousand people or she'd lose moments like this forever.

All she could do was her best and hope that it was enough. Hope that she and Hayley would be able to pull it off.

Olivia took off her eye patch.

Thankfully, the dim light of the moon didn't bother her eye.

Hopefully, her eye was getting better, and she wouldn't need the eye patch soon. She needed to remember to put the eye drops in when she got back to her cabin.

Olivia sighed at the beauty of the moonlight's silvery reflection on the waves.

She soaked in the view for a few seconds before she put the eye patch back on. She took one last deep breath of the salty air.

The door to the ship opened.

Olivia turned to see who was coming out on the deck of the ship in the middle of the night.

The dim light coming through the doorway silhouetted the person.

Olivia nodded to the dark figure and turned back towards the ocean.

The door shut behind them, leaving the deck dark again except for the light of the moon. The person stood in front of the door, their hand in their pocket jangling their change, as their eyes adjusted the dim light of the moon.

She wished they had gone to another part of the empty deck instead of coming near where she was standing.

A hand covered her mouth.

Olivia whipped around and grabbed her attackers forearms. She pushed against them.

They struggled, her attacker trying to lift her over the railing of the ship.

They tried to force her overboard, but they couldn't get her feet off the ground. Her attacker tried to shake Olivia's hands off of them, but she wouldn't let go. She used her straightened arms to keep them from getting closer to her.

Olivia shoved her attacker. They lurched backwards, stumbling in the dark.

Olivia held her breath, wondering if they were going to come at her again.

The person regained their footing and ran to door. They pulled it open and disappeared into the passageway.

Olivia's chest burned from holding her breath.

She looked up at the dark windows of the bridge, but couldn't see anyone in a white officer's uniform outlined in the dark windows.

Olivia was at the front of the ship with only the door her attacker had come through to get back inside.

Her heart pounded in her chest.

She looked up at the Bridge, but still couldn't see anyone. Even if she could, they probably couldn't make her out in the darkness. She knew that a lot of the crew came out on this deck at night with their dates to find a private, romantic place.

Even if they saw her from the Bridge, they wouldn't know she'd just been attacked.

She looked through the small window of the door. The passageway was dimly lit so the light wouldn't interfere with the officers on the bridge being able to see. The passageway intersected with another dimly lit hallway in a T.

Olivia could see the crew phone on the wall where the hallways met.

She took out her wallet, her hands shaking as she pulled out Alex's card.

Olivia took off her eye patch and put it in her pocket.

She took another deep breath, slowly pushed the door open, and stepped into the dark passageway.

18

Her steps echoed on the metal floor. Olivia slipped her shoes off. She quietly shut the door behind herself, trying to muffle the click of the lock in case her attacker was near. She crept towards the phone, glancing each way.

She reached for the phone and took it off the hook.

She dialed Alex's direct number.

He picked it up on the second ring.

"Officer Ballas." Alex's voice was gruff from sleep.

"Alex?" Olivia's voice was low and quiet.

"Yes."

"It's me. Olivia. Someone attacked me."

"Where are you?"

"I'm in the passage right behind the theatre. Under the Bridge, starboard side. I was out on the crew deck when I got jumped."

"Do I need to call Dr. Kohli?"

"No, I'm not hurt. Just shook up."

"I'll be right there. Don't move. Stay by the phone. Dial 17 for the Purser's desk if you hear anyone coming before I get there. It's staffed all night."

Olivia's chest heaved with quiet sobs.

"Olivia? Did you hear me?"

"Yes." Olivia's voice horse from strain.

The phone went dead in her hand. She hung up the phone, but gripped the handset in case she needed to call for help again.

Every creak of the ship made her tremble.

She startled as a door opened in the distance. The sound of feet in heavy shoes came towards her. Olivia flattened herself against the cold metal wall.

"Olivia!" Alex called out to her.

"Here."

Olivia let go of the phone, her legs shaking.

Alex charged around the corner, his radio crackling with static. He ran past her, pushed open the door to the deck, and shined his flashlight around the crew deck. He went back to the passageway he'd come down and looked both ways to make sure no one had followed him.

Alex came back to Olivia. She was shaking. The adrenaline left her system.

"Can you tell me what happened?"

Olivia's voice trembled. "Someone grabbed me and tried to throw me overboard."

"What did they look like?"

Olivia shook her head. "I could hardly see the person. There was just a dim outline in the doorway. I assumed it was someone coming out for some peace and quiet, like I had done."

"Your eyes had to have adjusted to the low light. You didn't see what they looked like when they came up behind you?"

"I couldn't see much because they were on the side of my eye patch."

"Can you tell me anything about them? Man or woman? How tall were they?" Alex asked.

"I... It all happened so fast. They covered my mouth with their hand. That's all I remember. I was too busy trying to stop them from throwing me overboard." Olivia shuddered.

"How did you stop them? You aren't that big."

"It was instinct. When they tried to pick me up, I did the Georgia Magnet." Olivia held her arms straight out in front of her and made a fist with each hand.

"Georgia Magnet? Is that an Americanism for punching someone?"

Olivia laughed for the first time since the attack. "No, it's an old Vaudeville trick. I used to do this bit when I first joined the magic act. We didn't have money to buy the big illusions, so I would do this trick in the show."

"You fought off the attacker with a magic trick?"

"Sort of. I did the 'Un-liftable girl'."

"The what?" Alex looked at her like she was speaking a foreign language.

"I held onto the person's forearms in such a way that they couldn't lift me to push me overboard. No matter how strong the person is who tries to lift the woman off the ground, they can't do it. Woman used to tour on Vaudeville, doing tricks like that in shows called The Georgia Magnet. I guess my body remembered what to do when the person grabbed me and tried to lift me over the railing."

Alex shook his head in disbelief. "I don't even know what to say about that. Why were you out on deck this late by yourself, anyway?"

"I wanted some quiet time." Olivia walked down the hall and picked up her shoes.

"Olivia, we've had two crew members killed. I've told you to be with someone at all times. Especially after stirring the pot."

She dropped the shoes on the ground and shoved her feet in them. "It was late. Hayley and I had been rehearsing, and she stayed to work on a trick. I figured the ship would be quiet at this time of night. I honestly didn't even think about it."

"Going out on deck by yourself in the middle of the night isn't a great thing to do ever, but doing it now, it is downright idiotic."

"Excuse me? Did you just call me an idiot?"

"Of course not. I meant it isn't safe to walk around the ship by yourself."

"Don't you walk around the ship at night by yourself?"

"Of course I do. It's part of my job. I'm a man and a security officer. I'm not a girl, all by herself."

"Alex, I am not a girl. I'm a full grown woman." Olivia's cheeks flushed. "I have spent years traveling around the world. I can take care of myself. I don't need you or any other man to keep me safe."

Alex rubbed his face with both hands. He sighed. "Olivia, you are the one who called me."

"I called you to report an incident. I handled it by myself, if you haven't noticed. The attacker is gone, and I didn't get thrown overboard." Olivia crossed her arms and looked at Alex defiantly. "Are we done?"

"We'll need to fill out an incident report, but we can do that in the morning. I'll walk you back to your cabin."

"I am perfectly capable of walking myself, thank you." Olivia glared at Alex.

"I am walking you to your cabin." Alex glared back.

"Fine." Olivia turned on her heal and stormed off towards her cabin.

Alex shook his head and walked behind her.

They reached the door to the passenger area. Olivia looked over her shoulder as she pushed open the heavy metal door. Alex reached above her head and helped push it open.

Olivia glared at him. "I didn't need your help."

"I know you didn't."

Alex looked around the lobby, making sure no one was waiting for Olivia there.

Olivia stopped and turned around. "Maybe you are the one that actually needs my help. Did you ever think about that?"

"What?" Alex asked.

"Aren't you supposed to be finding a murderer? Maybe I know things that would help you."

"Okay. Like what?"

"Like Anna was engaged to Emilio, but they didn't want people to know. Like Anna was up on the pool deck this afternoon and tore up a piece of paper and threw it overboard."

"And what does any of that have to do with the murders?"

"I think Anna killed Martin and Emilio."

"Anna? You think she is a murderer?"

"You don't think she could be a murderer because she's a girl. And a pretty one at that." Olivia sneered sarcastically.

"No, not because she's a 'girl' but because I haven't seen any evidence that made me think she killed either of them."

"She was fighting with Martin over her photos right before he died."

"According to you. She said she wasn't. She said she'd heard that Hayley was the one who had been fighting with him. Did you think I hadn't interviewed her?"

"Why would you believe her? If she is the murderer, she's going to lie."

"Believe it or not, part of my training is in recognizing deception."

"Funny, I'm trained in deception as part of my job, too."

Alex gave her a withering look. "A magician is not anything like a Security Officer."

Olivia glared at Alex. "Did Anna tell you she was engaged to Emilio?"

Alex shook his head. "No."

"Maybe you need to go over your training in deception and interview her again." Olivia pushed her cabin door open, gave him a withering glance, and slammed the door behind her.

"Holy Frijoles!"

"Sorry, Chico. I didn't mean to startle you. Up!" Chico stepped onto her hand . She rubbed his cheek feathers until they had both settled down.

19

Chico danced on his perch, looking out at the sea. He squeaked and bobbed his head up and down as a wave swept over the porthole.

Olivia sat at her desk, working on her patter for the show. She had always hated public speaking and struggled with memorization. Peter did all the talking in their show, so it hadn't mattered. Now, she was terrified she'd get on stage and forget everything, including her own name.

The cruise directors had introduced her as 'and his lovely assistant Olivia' for so long, she couldn't imagine being introduced as 'Olivia Morgan and her lovely assistant Hayley.'

"Ugh. I have to write an introduction for Tristan to use when he introduces us. Chico, give me some ideas."

Chico looked at her and cocked his head, but for once, was quiet.

"Thanks for nothing, birdie boy."

Chico tucked his foot in his breast feathers and made soft, sleepy noises.

Olivia wrote out the introduction she and Peter had used and changed his name to hers, and hers to Hayley's.

It didn't feel right.

Hayley hadn't been with them when they'd performed at the Magic Castle, so it was stretching things to use it.

She put her pen down and sat back. She didn't understand how one paragraph could be so hard to write. Olivia wanted the audience to be excited from the first moment of the show.

She ripped the paper off the pad and started over.

Olivia read her draft a couple of times and made some minor changes. She folded the paper and tucked it in the pocket of her sundress to show Hayley and get her opinion.

Olivia went back to her script.

Her cabin phone rang. She picked it up, expecting Hayley calling about meeting up for lunch.

"Hello?"

Chico chimed in with his own hello.

Olivia covered the phone with her hand. "Shh, Chico, be quiet. I can't hear." She put the receiver to her ear again.

"Sorry. Chico likes to say hello when the phone rings."

"Um, hello?"

"Sorry, this is Olivia."

"Olivia, this is Nigel. Tristan needs you to come to his office. Apparently, you had an incident last night, and he needs you to fill out the report with him."

"Oh, we don't need to do that. I'm ok."

"You know ships. All the paperwork. Don't have a choice. Can you come up to his office now?"

"Sure." She sighed and slumped in her chair. "I'll be there in a few minutes."

She was dreading telling Tristan about Peter leaving and her doing the show with Hayley. She should have told him as soon as she knew what had happened. He was going to be so angry with her. She had planned to tell him today, but now she couldn't put it off any longer.

"Alright Chico, wish me luck."

"Kerfuffle."

"Close enough."

Olivia knocked on Tristan's open door and walked in. Tristan was sitting at his desk.

"Hi, Nigel said you wanted to see me."

Tristan gestured to the man sitting across from him. "Alex told me what happened last night."

Alex turned in his chair and looked at Olivia. She felt awful at how rude she'd been to him. She had woken him up and hc had still come immediately to help her.

She nodded to him.

Tristan stood up and motioned for her to take a seat. "The attacker injured your eye?"

Olivia reached up and touched her eye patch. She'd forgotten she was wearing it. "Oh no, long story that involves a lorikeet wing, but no, the attacker didn't really hurt me. I have an appointment to see Dr. Kohli this afternoon for him to look at my eye. I should be able to take the patch off after that. It feels much better today."

"Good. Okay, tell me what happened so I can fill out these forms."

"Well, after I left Hayley rehearsing the levitation, I went out on the crew deck for a minute."

Tristan stopped writing. "Wait, why was Hayley rehearsing the levitation? Is she going to take over your part in the show tomorrow if Dr. Kohli doesn't clear you to return to duty?"

Olivia was kicking herself for not having told Tristan about Peter. Now she'd have to tell him in front of Alex, too.

"Hayley is subbing in for me in the show, but not because of my eye. She's doing my part of the show because I am doing Peter's part."

"Is Peter sick? Did he get hurt, too?"

"No. Peter is gone. He signed off the ship."

"What? When is he coming back?"

"He's not. Apparently, he and Candi signed off together. They're doing a show together on another cruise line."

"He can't do that. He's under contract."

"Well, he did it. I'm doing my best to honor our contract. That's why Hayley and I were rehearsing last night."

Tristan stood up and leaned across the desk towards Olivia. "You didn't think that Peter leaving was something I should know?"

"I did..." Olivia looked at Alex, but he was looking down at the notepad in his lap.

"I didn't know he'd left until we'd sailed. Hayley and I talked. We figured it would be hard to get another act out, so she offered to be my assistant. We've been diligently working all week to get the show reworked without Peter." Olivia held her breath, waiting to hear what Tristan would say.

Tristan picked up his phone. "Nigel, get Hayley Fensby up here, now."

They sat in uncomfortable silence until Hayley walked into the office.

"Hey all, how are you?"

Tristan's face turned beat red. "How am I? I'm not great. I found out I don't have a magic act for tomorrow night. That's how I am."

Hayley looked surprised. "You have a show. Olivia and me. I'm assuming Liv told you."

"She told me. Finally."

"We have it all handled, Tristan. It's going to be even better than her and Peter."

"Axis cruises hired their act because they had years of experience. They'd played all the top cruise lines and won awards. The entertainment director didn't hire a couple of dancers who threw together a show in less than a week."

Olivia felt crushed. Tristan was right. Who was she to think she could pull this off?

Hayley walked up to Tristan's desk, put her hands on it, and leaned towards him. "For your information, Olivia played all the top cruise lines just as much as Peter did. Last I checked, Olivia's name is engraved on the same awards that Peter's is."

"Be that as it may, I will talk to the comedian and get him to do another show tomorrow night. Most of the comedians have a lot more time they can do than they use on this run. They have to have at least two 45 minute shows for the 10 and 14 day cruises. Olivia, I'll need you to work on the manifest to ship the illusions to your home when we get back to port. Can you get the vet arranged to sign your parrot off as well?"

Hayley shifted her feet and crossed her arms. "You're firing her? Well, if you're firing her, then I quit. Good luck with the revue show tonight. You know, the one that starts in just a few hours. I'm sure it'll be great without a lead singer."

Tristan sat back in his chair and folded his arms.

Hayley sat on the arm of Olivia's chair. Olivia put her hand on Hayley's hand to get her to stop, but Hayley pushed her away. "We aren't a couple of dancers. We're professional entertainers. I've performed on Broadway, remember? And you should remember that Olivia performed at The Magic Castle since you say it in her intro every show. I'm confident that we're more than capable of putting together a stellar show."

"Really? Confident enough that it won't bother you that Gayle Rogers, the Entertainment Director for the entire fleet, is on the ship and will be in the audience for your show tomorrow night?"

Olivia's heart dropped, and she felt all the air leave her lungs. An odd squeak sound escaped her mouth.

"Yes, we are plenty confident." Hayley reached for Olivia's hand and squeezed it. "Actually, this is wonderful. She'll get to see what we're capable of, right Olivia?"

"Right." Olivia tried to sound confident.

Tristan looked from Hayley to Olivia and back to Hayley. Hayley smiled at him as if she didn't have a care in the world.

"I hope you are right. If you fall flat on your faces, you'll be taking me down with you. Olivia, you need to go see Dr. Kohli and get cleared to perform. None of this will matter if Olivia isn't fit to do the show."

"Ready to answer the questions?" Alex picked up the incident report.

Olivia nodded.

Tristan stood up. "Hayley, why don't we leave them to that?"

"Yes, sir!" Hayley leaned down and whispered to Olivia. "If you need me, come find me, okay?"

Alex and Olivia filled out the rest of the incident report. "I'd appreciate it if you could stay out of trouble. I'm getting pretty tired of the paperwork."

"I didn't go looking for trouble. I was minding my business."

"This time."

Olivia glared at Alex. Her regret for how she'd talked to him the previous evening vanishing. "So, are we done?"

"Not quite. You need to be checked over by Dr. Kohli. I'll walk you to the infirmary."

"Thanks, but I know where it is."

"I know you do." Alex looked pointedly at her eye patch. "But I need to add his evaluation to my report."

They took the crew elevator down to the infirmary in total silence.

Dr. Kohli looked at Olivia with concern. "Ah, Olivia. Our appointment isn't until later this afternoon. Is your eye giving you trouble? Did the drops not help?"

"Actually, Dr. Kohli, my eye feels much better. Thank you. I'm hoping you'll give me the okay to go without the eye patch, but that's not why I'm here."

Dr. Kohli motioned for Alex and Olivia to sit down. "What can I help you with, my dear?"

"Well, Dr. Kohli. Someone attacked me last night. They tried to push me overboard."

"Oh, my poor dear! Are you alright?"

"Yes, thankfully. But Alex and Tristan want you to check me over as part of the incident report."

"Of course, come back to the exam room."

Alex stood up and walked with them.

Olivia turned towards him. "No way. You are not coming into the exam room. You stay out here."

"I wasn't going into the exam room. I was going to sit in the waiting room instead of Dr. Kohli's office."

"Oh, sorry."

Olivia followed Dr. Kohli and sat on top of the exam table. He asked her about the attack and where she'd been injured.

"I was shook up, but thankfully, I am not hurt."

"How did you fend off the attacker and not get injured?"

Olivia explained how she'd used the 'un-liftable girl' magic trick so the attacker couldn't pick her up.

Dr. Kohli nodded, "Ah yes, I've seen street magicians in my country do similar tricks."

"I really am fine. If you could double check my eye and then tell Alex that I'm ok for his report, that would be great."

"I need to look you over. Any bruising?"

"A little here." Olivia pointed to some bruising. "It doesn't hurt much. Not more than I get learning a new magic trick."

"You said that your attacker put their hand over your mouth?"

Olivia nodded.

"Did they hurt your neck or head when they grabbed you like that?"

Olivia turned her head to the left and then to the right. "No, my neck doesn't hurt. I think I surprised them when I turned towards them so quickly. Their hands were trying to stop me from grabbing their forearms so they didn't have their hands over my mouth for long."

Olivia replayed that moment in her mind and felt tears overflowing her eyes. "Oh! I just remembered something! I need to tell Alex."

Olivia jumped off the exam table.

"Alex!" Olivia burst through the waiting room door. "I remembered something about the attacker."

"Their hands had a funny smell when they covered my mouth. I couldn't place it at the time. But I think I know what it was. They had a metallic smell."

"Are you sure?" Alex asked.

"Yes. I think their hand smelled like metal or coins."

Alex lifted the clipboard with the incident report. "I'll add that to the report."

"Oh, for goodness' sake. Don't you get it? You know who handles a lot of coins? Casino workers."

Olivia put her hands on her hips. "Anna. Working in the casino, she's constantly in contact with coins and tokens. I knew it. I told you to interview her again."

20

Alex stood up and stepped towards her. "Do not tell me how to do my job."

"Why not? You keep telling me what to do."

Olivia's hands shook. Instead of telling her what to do, he needed to be doing his job, finding the killer. She thought better of saying this to Alex out loud.

Dr. Kohli cleared his throat. "So, Olivia. I found nothing that would prevent you from completing your duties. You are free to take off the eye patch. Good luck with your show tomorrow night."

"Thank you. I appreciate you checking me over." Olivia took the eye patch off and tucked it into the pocket of her sundress.

"I'll send you my written report, Alex." Dr. Kohli shook Alex's hand and patted him on the shoulder.

"Thank you, sir. I'll forward a copy of your report with my incident report to Tristan and the Captain."

Olivia and Alex walked up the crew stairs to Olivia's deck. She nodded at him and walked towards her cabin. After a few steps, she heard someone behind her. She turned and looked. Alex was walking ten feet behind her.

"You can't follow me everywhere, you know."

"No, but I can make sure you get safely to your cabin."

Olivia rolled her eyes and continued to her cabin. She got to her door, swiped her key card, and opened her door.

"Hey, Baby!"

Alex stood in the hallway. "Hello, Chico. How are you today?"

Chico danced back and forth on his perch. He bobbed his head up and down.

Olivia gave Alex a tight-lipped smile and shut her cabin door.

"You don't have to be so excited to see him, you know?" Olivia picked Chico up and cuddled him to her chest.

Rays of sunlight cut across the near empty atrium.

"Hello, Miss Olivia." Joseph was polishing the brass handrails around the circular staircase.

"Oh, Joseph. Hi. How are you?"

"Could be worse, I guess. How are you?"

Joseph dunked his rag in a can of polish and rubbed his cloth on the brass railing. He took a clean rag and wiped off the polish.

"Okay, I guess. See you later."

Olivia walked away, but couldn't get the picture of Joseph cleaning the brass railing out of her head. She wondered if that could make his hands smell like metal.

The purser's desk was quiet. Olivia looked for Sophie.

She popped her head up over the desk. "Oh! Sorry! Bit of a disaster back here, mate."

Olivia looked over the desktop and saw a blonde head bent over a pile of coins on the floor. The person was picking up the coins and putting them into the proper slots in the cash drawer.

"What happened? Anything I can do to help?"

"Nah, we've got it. I accidentally dropped the cash drawer."

Anna looked up at her and glared.

Olivia gasped.

"No worries. Anna's helping me pick up the mess and get it back in the drawer. Heard you had a bit of a scare last night."

"How did you know?" Olivia asked.

Anna continued picking up the change.

"Tristan told me." Sophie knelt down to help Anna.

"Ah. Okay. Well, I had better run and let you get your drawer picked up."

Olivia ran down the stairs to her cabin. She threw open her cabin door and slammed it shut behind her. She leaned on her door and let out a sigh.

Chico opened one eye, looked at her reproachfully for waking him up from his nap. He muttered under his breath at her.

"Sorry I disturbed you. A little freaked out about all the potential murders around the ship."

"Fiddlesticks."

Olivia glared at him. "You can keep your opinions to yourself, sir."

Olivia looked up. "You are doing really well, Hayley. Take deep breaths. Are you ready?"

"I'd nod, but I don't want to start this sucker shaking."

From stage left, in the dark, a voice rang out. "Hello?"

Chico squawked. "Phooey."

Blake walked into the light of the stage. "Oh sorry. Didn't mean to interrupt."

"Hayley, hang on. I'll get you down and we can try again in a minute."

Olivia quickly lowered Hayley down to the ground and turned towards to Blake.

"Sorry, I didn't want to leave her hanging up there."

"No problem. I was coming to see how you were doing."

Hayley yawned. "Sorry, I did the production show and then rehearsal. It's been a long night."

Olivia looked at Hayley. "I'm so sorry. This is too much for you."

"No, I'm fine." Hayley looked expectantly at Blake, waiting for him to leave so they could finish their rehearsal.

"Olivia, you look lovely."

Olivia looked down at her costume. "Thanks."

"Oh, you don't have the eye patch on!"

"Yes, thankfully, Dr. Kohli said I didn't need it any-more."

"Good news."

Chico flapped his wing, blowing her hair into her face. Olivia tucked her hair behind her ear. "Slow down, dude!"

Chico stopped flapping. "Crud."

Hayley yawned again and covered her mouth with the back of her hand. "I'm sorry!"

Olivia laughed. "Hayley, you need to get to bed and get some rest, so you'll be able to do the show tomorrow."

"We need to finish the rehearsal."

"It's late. Tomorrow is a sea day. We can come in here after Bingo and do a run through. Go to bed and we'll meet back up then."

"I promised Alex I wouldn't leave you here alone."

Olivia shook her head. "I don't need babysitting, Hayley."

Blake looked at Hayley. "Olivia won't be alone. I'll stay with her."

Hayley rolled her eyes and laughed. "Ah yes, I get it. Don't worry about me. I'll head out and give you two privacy."

Olivia rolled her eyes. "You know that's not what I meant."

"Yes, Livvy, I know that isn't what you meant." Hayley leaned in to hug Olivia and whispered in her ear. "But I think it is what Blake meant."

Hayley winked at Olivia as she picked up her bag. Her strings of sequins and strands of rhinestones swaying as she walked towards the dressing room.

"You don't have to stay. Contrary to what Hayley said, I'm perfectly capable of staying here alone and getting my work done."

"I know how capable you are." Blake put his hand in his pocket and jangled his keys. "Why doesn't Alex want you here alone?"

"He thinks I've asked too many questions about the murders." Olivia sat on the edge of the illusion case and put Chico down on the case so he could run around while she folded another copy of her newspaper trick. Chico rocked back and forth, muttering to himself.

"What does the demise of Martin and Emilio have to do with you?" Blake asked.

"Hayley is one of the suspects. I know she didn't do it, so I want to help figure out who did."

"Why are you so sure she didn't?"

Olivia looked at Blake in shock. "How could you think that? She's my best friend. I know she wouldn't kill anyone."

Blake shrugged. "I heard Martin was a bit of a rogue. Maybe he took it a step too far with Hayley. She is a beautiful woman."

"Hayley handled Martin's flirtation with more grace than I would have. It is not even a possibility that Hayley would have killed him." Olivia crossed her arms.

"If you know she couldn't possibly have done it, why don't you just let it go? It is not your job to investigate. Leave it to Ballas."

"I don't need to figure out who the killer was just for Hayley. I need to figure out for me. Someone attacked me last night."

Blake leaned towards her. "Who attacked you?"

"I don't know." Olivia explained to Blake how someone had tried to throw her overboard the night before.

Blake shrugged his shoulders. "Huh, maybe someone was trying to play a practical joke on you?"

Chico waddled towards Blake, his orange eyes pinning. Blake looked down at Chico and took a step back.

"Well, if they were, it sure didn't feel funny. Thankfully, I handled it."

"Yes, you did. With all of your questioning, do you think you have come any closer to knowing what happened?"

Chico flapped his wings and swayed back and forth.

"I wish." Olivia shrugged.

"I have to say I agree with Ballas. You need to drop it and move on."

"It would be nice to not have to watch my back everywhere I go, worried that I'm going to be attacked."

"That must be very stressful for you."

Olivia nodded. "Yes, especially on top of trying to get the show right for tomorrow night."

"Ah, yes, yours and Hayley's big debut. I can't wait to see it."

"Bad boy!" Chico squawked.

Blake walked around the stage so that Olivia sat between him and Chico.

Olivia wagged her finger at Chico in reproach. "That's enough. You're scaring Blake."

"He's not scaring me."

Blake took a step closer and Chico lunged at him.

Blake leapt backwards.

"Damn bird. Stop it."

"Seriously, he's a gentle bird. All bark, no bite."

Chico barked like a dog.

"He won't hurt you."

Olivia walked over to the stage curtain and opened it. "I'll put him on the ring stand we use during the opening of the show."

She walked over to Chico and put her hand down by his belly. "Up."

Chico stepped on her hand. She took him to the stage apron and put him on the ring stand. She reached into her pocket and pulled out a walnut and handed it to him. "That'll keep you busy for a bit."

Chico settled in to work opening his nut.

Olivia walked over to the Substitution Trunk illusion and opened the lid. She reached in and reset the trick, putting the cuffs and key in her pocket.

"Sorry, I need to get everything reset for tomorrow."

"No rush. I'm not scheduled until 11 tomorrow." Blake glanced at Chico across the stage. He nervously fiddled with the change in his pocket.

"You don't have to stay. I have a few more things I have to reset before I can leave. I'll be fine on my own."

"Oh no. I promised to stay with you." Blake walked up to Olivia and lifted his hand to her cheek. Blake tilted his head and reached in to kiss her.

Olivia pulled away.

"Kiss me." Blake pulled her in towards him. He cupped her face with both of his hands and kissed her.

Olivia closed her eyes and leaned in. She kissed him back and breathed in his scent.

His hands smelled of money.

The memory of her attacker putting their hand over her mouth rushed over her.

Olivia froze.

The metallic scent. The jangling of the coins in his pocket.

Olivia gasped and looked at Blake.

He saw the change in her eyes.

Olivia tried to pull away, but he gripped her arms, not letting her go.

"It's you. You did it. You tried to throw me overboard." She stiffened. "You killed Martin and Emilio."

Blake's nostrils flared. "You have no proof of anything."

Chico yelled and flapped his wings. "Ah, ah! Ah!"

"Shut up bird!"

"It was you in Martin's picture." Olivia tried to pull away from Blake, but he grabbed her tighter.

"What picture?" Blake's voice was low and threatening.

"I found the pictures of Martin and Emilio. That was you in his pictures, wasn't it?"

Blake's nostrils flared. "I looked everywhere for those pictures, but I couldn't find them. I figured he'd given them to Emilio. Martin couldn't keep his mouth shut."

"You killed him. You killed them both." Olivia tried to twist her arm out of his grasp.

"Martin thought he was so clever, blackmailing me with pictures of me with the money I'd skimmed. He wanted a cut. That was my money. I figured out how to take it and not get caught. Why would I give him any of it? I got him fired off our last ship." Sweat beaded up on Blake's forehead. "If he'd just stayed off ships, I wouldn't have had to do this."

Blake loosened his grip on her arms. His eyes stared blankly past Olivia.

"I join this ship and the first person I see is Martin. He told me he was going to go to the Captain if I didn't pay him. I was done being blackmailed." Blake sneered. His fingers dug into Olivia's arm. "He was going to expose me. I couldn't let that happen, now could I?"

Olivia shook her head.

Olivia turned pale. "You're a murderer."

Blake slapped Olivia.

Chico launched himself off his perch and flew at Blake. He landed on Blake's shoulder and bit him on the ear. Blake let go of Olivia and grabbed his ear.

"You little beast." Blake smacked Chico with the back of his hand, launching him across the stage.

Olivia used the moment of distraction to wrench her arm away from Blake.

Chico landed on a seat in the first row in the auditorium.

"Uh oh! Oh no!" Chico yelled.

Olivia ran towards the dressing room door. Blake came after her.

He grabbed her arm and yanked her back.

"I made a mistake not throwing Martin and Emilio overboard after I killed them. Their bodies never would have been found. I won't make that mistake again."

Chico flapped his wings and flew through the theatre. He landed on the floor by the entrance. His wings drooped and he was out of breath. He waddled through the door at the theatre entrance and into the lobby.

"Uh oh! Oh no!"

The crew doorway swung open.

Alex looked down at Chico waddling across the carpeted floor of the lobby.

"Hello?" Chico looked up at Alex. "Hello, uh oh!"

Alex bent down to Chico. "What on earth are you doing out here? I can't imagine it will please Olivia that you are on the loose."

He put his hand in front of Chico. Chico jumped onto Alex's hand. He was panting. "Oh No! Bad Boy! Bad, bad boy!"

"Are you a bad boy for leaving the theatre? Well, I'll take you back to Olivia. I'm sure she'll be relieved to see that you are safe." Chico climbed up Alex's arm and onto his shoulder. "I just finished my rounds and was coming to check on her and Hayley. I didn't know I was going to find you on a little adventure."

Alex heard a scream coming from the stage. He ran through the entrance.

Olivia struggled to get away from Blake.

Alex raced down the aisle towards the stage.

Chico flapped his wings, lost his grip on Alex's shoulder, and flew down to the back of a chair.

Blake grabbed Olivia's throat, choking her.

She grabbed his arms and tried to pry them loose.

Blake gripped her tighter.

Olivia struggled to breathe. She tried to pull his hands off her neck.

Blake squeezed her neck tighter.

Olivia's arms dropped to her side. She sank to the ground.

Blake lurched forward, thrown off balance, as her weight pulled on him.

Alex reached the first row. He grabbed the edge of the stage and launched himself up and over onto the stage.

Blake turned towards Alex.

Alex reached for his taser.

Blake pulled Olivia's limp body in front of him, using her as a shield.

Olivia whipped around, snapped a handcuff onto his wrist, closing the other on the handle of the Substitution Trunk. He pulled against the heavy trunk but couldn't get it to move more than a few inches at time.

Blake sank to the stage floor and leaned back against the trunk. His hand hooked to the trunk lid.

Alex slowed. Olivia ran to him.

She leaned in close and whispered in his ear, "The handcuffs are friction cuffs, trick handcuffs. Use your handcuffs before he realizes it."

Alex eyes widened and he raced to Blake. He took his handcuffs off his belt and quickly cuffed Blake.

"Hello?" Chico waddled up to the stage. "Uh oh! Oh no!!!"

Alex smiled. "Chico did a good thing going for help."

"He did." She walked to the stairs on the edge of the stage. "Chico doesn't like being on the floor. He wants me to pick him up."

"Up!" Chico fluttered his wings, begging to be picked up

Olivia reached down for him. "He's too chunky to fly to me from the floor."

Chico looked at Olivia and bobbed his head up and down. "Treat?"

O livia threw her makeup in her makeup case and slammed the lid shut. She pulled Chico's travel carrier out from under her bed and put him in it.

She took a deep breath, trying to calm herself.

The craziness of last night had made her forget about the show for a while, but now, the countdown to the start of the show was closing in on her.

She headed out the door, wrestling Chico's carrier and her makeup case through her cabin door, using her hip to keep it open.

She dropped her key card.

Olivia put the carrier and makeup case down and picked the key card up off the floor.

Down the hall, a door opened, and Joseph crept out of a cabin.

He saw her and put his hand over his heart. "Oh miss. You startled me."

"Are you alright, Joseph?"

Joseph looked both ways down the passage. "Can you keep a secret?"

"I guess."

"Come see. There was a bird that landed on the deck of the ship. I've been keeping him in this empty cabin. I'm going to release him when we got back to port."

Olivia put Chico's carrier and her makeup case back in her cabin and closed her door.

Joseph gestured for her to follow him into the cabin.

Joseph opened up a crate. A grey and white bird with black feathers on his head and an orange beak sat huddled in the corner of the crate.

Olivia covered her mouth with her hand. "Oh, my goodness."

"I must apologize. I took some of Chico's food to see if he would eat it, but he wouldn't."

Olivia smiled. "You could have just asked me. I wouldn't have minded."

"I know, miss, so sorry. If anyone found out, I was afraid they would take the bird off the ship someplace away from his family. I know how much I miss my family and I get to go home at the end of my contract. I didn't want that to happen to him."

"You're a good man, Joseph." Olivia looked at the bird. His breathing was labored. "So, what have you been feeding him?"

"Well, when Chico's food didn't work, I brought other things to try. He didn't like fruit or vegetables, but he gulped down some fish that a passenger left on their room service tray."

"That makes sense. I think he's a tern. They eat fish and some insects."

"Yes, I think that is it. I brought him shrimp, and he ate it all." Joseph looked at her and cocked his head. "Maybe I need to look for some bugs for him."

Olivia giggled. "Can't hurt!"

"You will not tell anyone, will you? I don't want anything bad to happen to him."

"Of course not, Joseph. Your secret is safe with me."

"Hayley, I am so sorry we didn't get to do another run through."

Hayley cocked one eyebrow. "Are you kidding? You captured a killer last night. You've had a pretty full plate."

"I still feel bad. I don't want to let you down."

"Liv, there isn't anything you could do that would let me down. Okay? No pressure. We'll go out and do our best and have as much fun as we can have. If we mess up, we'll just keep going. The show must go on, right?"

Olivia fist bumped Hayley. "Sounds like a plan."

Tristan peaked into the dressing room. "Five minutes. Are you ladies ready?"

Hayley stood up, her long leg peaking out of the slit in her velvet dress. She put her hand on her hip and flashed Tristan a crooked smile. "Oh yes. We're so ready."

"Glad to hear it. Gayle Rogers is sitting in the front row." Tristan closed the curtain on his way to the stage.

Olivia put Chico into his trick and looked at Hayley. "Are we really ready?"

"It's opening night. Is anyone ever really ready for an opening night?"

Olivia and Hayley stood in the dark. A line of light peaked under the heavy red curtain in front of them. The light swayed with the waves. Tristan stood in front of the curtain, reciting their introduction.

Olivia's heart pounded to the rhythm of their opening music.

Tristan's voice rose as he drew out every syllable. "Welcome to stage, Olivia Morgan and Hayley."

The curtain opened.

The light of the follow spot hit Olivia. She looked at Hayley.

Hayley gave her a small nod.

Olivia took a step forward and raised her hand in the air. In a flash of fire, Chico was perched on her hand. He flapped his wings to the audience's applause.

Hayley took Chico from Olivia and ran backstage as the red curtains closed, leaving Olivia alone in the circle of light in front of the audience. She tore her newspaper into small pieces and folded it into a bundle.

Olivia looked out into the darkened auditorium, only the first few rows of faces visible. Gayle Rogers sat in the center of the front row. She had a notepad in her lap and was taking notes.

Olivia took a deep breath. She grabbed the edges of the newspaper and shook it open. The audience clapped as it unfurled, completely restored. She sighed in relief.

The curtains swooshed open behind her and Hayley came back out on stage with Chico. He and Hayley sang their songs to the audience's delight.

Hayley and Chico took their bows and headed backstage. Olivia stood in the center with her silver rings. She linked and unlinked them in rhythm to the music. She slid five of them up her arm into the crook of her elbow, and held two linked rings in front of her face. Olivia rubbed them together and slowly separated them. She lifted the two rings above her head and then dropped her arms down. One ring fell and rolled across the stage towards Hayley standing in the wings.

Olivia's heart dropped, and her cheeks burned.

Hayley gracefully entered the stage, swept up the ring, and spun it around in her hands before dancing her way to Olivia.

Olivia finished the routine, linked the rings to each other, and held the seven linked rings above her head.

She grinned at Hayley as the audience applauded.

The levitation music began.

Hayley took a deep breath. She nodded. She was ready.

Olivia and Hayley moved into place.

Olivia gestured towards Hayley, and Hayley went limp. Hayley's upstage hand was clenched in a fist, but she looked asleep as she rose from the stage.

Olivia held her breath, hoping Hayley could stay calm and not panic.

The music soared. The stage lights followed Hayley as she rose further from the ground.

Hayley floated to the top of the levitation.

Olivia lifted the large silver hoop and swished it over Hayley, showing that she was floating unsupported.

The audience clapped.

Olivia gestured toward Hayley. She seemed to come awake and stretched, moving her arms and legs, free from any tethers.

Olivia stepped back and held the silver hoop as if she was going to throw it towards Hayley. As she threw it, the hoop vanished and Chico appeared. He flew from Olivia's hand up to Hayley. He flapped his wings as Hayley descended back onto the stage.

Olivia took Hayley's right hand and Chico perched on Hayley's left. The three of them walked to the front of the stage, the audience clapping.

Olivia and Hayley took a bow and then ran off stage.

Olivia hugged Hayley as the audience continued to clap.

Tristan called them back on stage. They ran to the center stage and took another bow.

Chico flew from Hayley's hand, circled over the audience's heads. He flew a lap around the auditorium and landed on Olivia's outstretched hand.

The clapping audience rose to their feet. Olivia and Hayley took another bow and then backed up. The curtained closed in front of them and a hush fell over the stage.

Olivia grinned at Hayley as they walked back to the dressing room.

"We did it. I didn't know if we could, but we did it."

"Gadzooks!" Chico shook out his feathers and looked at Olivia expectantly.

"Yes, I know. You want your treat. Here you go, buddy."

Tristan knocked on their dressing room door. "Is everyone decent?"

"Yes, come in on."

Tristan walked in with a woman.

Olivia stood up to great them.

"Olivia, Hayley, you know our entertainment director, Gayle Rogers."

"Ladies, I couldn't wait to come back and meet you both." Gayle reached out and shook their hands. "I've been in this business for twenty years and I have never seen an act like yours. I love that you are a female magician, Olivia. The world needs more women in non-traditional roles. And that bird! He's a star. If I have any advice to give you, it's add more Chico!"

Chico cocked his head at his name. "Oh, boy!"

"Cheers." Olivia lifted her glass and clinked Hayley's.

Hayley took a sip of her drink. "You were amazing. When the curtain opened, it was like a light bulb lit up inside of you. You glowed from within. It was wonderful seeing your confidence come back."

"Its been a heck of a week. Hard to feel confident when your boyfriend dumps you, you almost get thrown overboard, and you almost date a murderer."

"You fought off an attacker, and you took down the murderer. I think you're pretty amazing."

"One thing that this week has confirmed is that I have the worst taste in men."

"You're a good person, so you don't look at people around you expecting them to be cheaters or murderers."

"Or I'm naïve. Either way, I'm done with men."

J oseph opened the crate. He and Olivia stood back and waited. The bird hopped up on the edge of the crate and looked around. He launched himself off the crate and flew towards land.

"Thank you for helping me, miss."

"Glad to help. It was pretty wonderful to see him fly back to his home."

"Yes, it was. Well, I've got to get back and get the cabins cleaned for the new passengers."

Olivia knocked on Hayley's door. "The ship's docked. Are you ready to run some errands?"

Hayley's door opened up and Tristan walked out.

"Hello, Olivia. Excellent job last night." He walked away down the passageway.

Olivia looked at Hayley. "I see that you aren't done with men."

"I never said I was." Hayley grinned. "But it isn't like that. He came by to tell me he was sorry for doubting me when I said we could do it. He's thrilled our show went well."

"Hmm, he didn't come to my cabin to tell me that."

"Anyway..." Hayley rolled her eyes. "Are your ready to do a week's worth of errands in six hours and then do this all again?"

"All but the murder part!"

Hayley and Olivia walked to the crew gangway.

Alex stood with his clipboard, signing paperwork. He handed it to two Coast Guard officers. They grabbed Blake by his handcuffed arms and walked him off the ship.

Olivia, Hayley, and Alex watched them put Blake in a waiting car.

"Good to see him gone."

Alex caught Olivia's eye and nodded. "Good work last night. You guys did great."

"You watched the show?"

"Of course. I wanted to see what you did with your trick handcuffs."

Olivia laughed and put her finger to her lips. "Shh. Don't tell my secrets."

Alex shook his head and laughed. "I won't. Even knowing that, I couldn't figure out how you did your tricks. Maybe I'll figure it out if I watch your show again next cruise."

"Next cruise, we don't have to worry about murders. We can just relax."

Anna walked up to them. "I heard what happened. I'm glad you are safe, Olivia."

"I'm very sorry for your loss, Anna."

"We were supposed to get married, you know. We even had our marriage license. When I told him about the pictures Martin took of me, he broke up with me. He said horrible things to me. I don't even know how to feel."

"Oh, Anna. I am so sorry." Olivia hugged her. Tears poured down Anna's cheeks as she walked off the ship.

"Ready?" Hayley nodded towards the doorway.

Olivia and Hayley walked down the gangway towards the line of taxis, the warm sun on their faces. It felt good to be on solid ground.

"Olivia!"

Olivia stopped dead in her tracks. "Peter?"

"I've made a terrible mistake."

Would you like to get the prequel e-book for this series for free? Join my newsletter!

Gotcha! is the story of how Olivia came to adopt Chico, her adorable, talkative parrot!

In my newsletters, I share my writing news, a little bit about me and my life as an author, my new releases, and if my books go on sale.

Visit https://wendyneugent.com/free-book/ to sign up for my newsletter and get your free ebook.

Happy Reading!

Wendy

If you enjoyed this book, please consider leaving a review.

Enjoy this sneak peek of Pier Pressure, the next book in the Olivia Morgan Cruise Ship Mystery Series.

"Olivia, I've made a terrible mistake." Peter reached out his arms, waiting for Olivia to run to him.

A blue sky had greeted Hayley and Olivia as they had walked off the gangway of their cruise ship. Olivia shivered at the sudden drop in temperature as a dark cloud passed in front of the sun, covering them in its shadow.

Olivia froze. Her cheeks flushed pink in the tropical sun. She took a deep breath of the humid air, filled with the briny scent of the ocean water.

"Olivia?" Peter glanced up at the massive cruise ship docked next to them.

Her eyes darted toward her best friend, Hayley.

Hayley shrugged, her eyes wide.

"Peter." Olivia clenched her jaw. "What are you doing here?"

"I shouldn't have left." Peter shoved his hands in the pockets of his shorts and looked down at the ground.

Olivia's heart beat so hard she wondered if he could see it pounding beneath her sundress. She crossed her arms.

"What are you doing here?"

"I'm here to sign back on the ship."

"Things didn't work out with Candi?"

Peter's jaw dropped, and his eyes darted around, avoiding Olivia. "Oh, you know about her?"

"Sure do." A breeze blew her skirt. She reached down to keep it from blowing up.

Hayley touched Olivia's shoulder. "I'm going to give you two some privacy. If you need me, I'll be over on that bench."

Olivia nodded at Hayley but didn't take her eyes off Peter.

He shuffled his feet.

Olivia waited.

Peter glanced at her before looking back down at the concrete dock. He took a deep breath. "Look, can't we just forget that this past week happened and go back to normal?"

Olivia let out a thin gasp of a laugh. "Ha! Normal? You mean when I was living in ignorance that you were a lying, cheating....."

"Come on, babe. We're good together. I just made a mistake."

"A mistake? A mistake is when you grab the wrong carton and pour orange juice on your cereal instead of milk." Olivia clenched her fists. "It's not cheating on your girlfriend, who is also your business partner, and then abandoning her on the cruise ship with a show scheduled in less than a week."

Olivia walked away from Peter. He followed her and put his hand on her shoulder. Olivia whipped around. "Keep your hands off of me."

"Liv. Don't be like this. I said I made a mistake. I love you, baby. Come on. We're so good together."

"I am not your baby. Never call me that again. As a matter of fact, don't ever call me anything again. We are done." Olivia glared at Peter.

Peter ran his hand through his dark, thinning hair. "Ok, don't be so sensitive. Everyone makes mistakes. What we have is really good."

"I thought it was good at the time, but in hindsight, it wasn't very good at all."

"Ah, baby..." Peter caught himself. "Sorry. Olivia. What do I have to say to you for you to get past this?"

Olivia looked at Hayley sitting on the bench, waiting for her. "Peter. There isn't anything you can say. This past week has been eye-opening for me. I've learned a lot about myself, and one thing I have learned is that I don't need you. I am a perfectly capable woman all on my own."

"What about our show? You need me for that. It's not like you can do it on your own."

"There is no 'our' show anymore."

The wind died down, leaving the air heavy.

Olivia smoothed her skirt. A trickle of sweat ran down her forehead. She wiped it away from her eyes.

"I can get another assistant. But what are you going to do without me?" Peter rocked on his heels and crossed his arms. "You need me way more than I need you, Olivia."

"Ha! Is that what you think? Interesting." Olivia crossed her arms. "I seemed to have done just fine this past cruise without you."

"What do you mean? You did fine without me? Did you get a job as cruise staff or something?" Peter's brows knit together.

"No. I didn't get another job on the ship." Olivia stood up tall, her shoulders pushed back. "I mean, I performed my show for the audience."

"Your show? You don't have a show." Peter scoffed. "You're just my assistant."

Olivia took a deep breath and slowly let it out. "You know, a week ago, I would have agreed with you. But it turns out that I'm not just your assistant. I learned that I can do this without you."

Peter shook his head. "I'm sorry. I really don't understand. Are you saying you performed our magic show without me?"

Olivia nodded. "Yes, that is exactly what I mean."

Peter snorted and shook his head. "That must have been really something. Does Tristan have a new act scheduled to come on today to replace you?"

"No. He liked what I did. I'm finishing out the contract."

Peter tilted his head and laughed. "Oh, I get it. You're sleeping with the cruise director."

Olivia's eyes blazed, and her mouth hung open. "You have got to be kidding me. No, I'm not sleeping with him. I put on a really good magic show. We got a standing ovation."

"We?" Peter raised his eyebrows.

"Yes, we. Hayley, Chico. and I."

Peter glared at Hayley. He snorted. "So Hayley saved you, huh?"

"No, Peter. I saved myself. I am done with this conversation." Olivia walked towards Hayley.

Peter followed her. "I'm going to talk to Tristan and get him to sign me back on. When he does, we'll discuss whether I'll keep you on as my assistant or not."

Olivia nodded towards the ship. "He's coming down the crew gangway right now. Here is your opportunity."

Peter stormed towards the gangway.

Olivia sat next to Hayley on the bench. She looked up at the clouds racing across the sky.

Hayley took a deep breath and let it out. "Did you take him back?"

Olivia's eyes widened. "Are you kidding me? You think I would take that sorry excuse for a man back?"

Hayley smiled. "When I asked you what you would do if he came back, you said you didn't know. You didn't want to waste all the years you had invested in your relationship with him."

"Yep, you are right. I said that. But now, I know who he is. I'm not throwing good years after bad."

Hayley took Olivia's hand and squeezed it. "Good for you, sis."

Peter walked towards them, sweat trickling down his red forehead. "Hayley, can you give us a minute?"

Hayley stood up. "No, Hayley is welcome to stay." Olivia stood up and grabbed Hayley's arm.

"Fine." Peter clenched his fists. "Tristan said that he and the entertainment director want you to finish the contract."

Olivia looked at Hayley and grinned.

Peter shifted uncomfortably. "So, I guess you need to go on the ship and fill out the paperwork to sign off my illusions."

"Your illusions?" Olivia tilted her head. "The ones you left on the ship?"

"Well, of course. You didn't think you were going to keep all of my stuff, did you?"

"We bought all the props for the show together. For our show. It is not all yours, Peter."

"I bought it all for my career."

"With the money we made doing our show. I'm not just giving it all to you. It's just as much mine as it is yours."

"I will get my illusions back and that bird, too." Peter pursed his lips.

Olivia shook her head. "Chico is my parrot. I paid for him with my money that I inherited when my dad passed. My name, and only my name, is on his paperwork."

Peter's nostrils flared. "Fine."

Olivia stood up and put her hands on her hips. "I'll sign off half of the magic equipment next week. Come here and it will be waiting for you on the dock. You can arrange your own shipping."

Peter opened his mouth to answer and then closed it again. "You can expect to hear from my attorney."

He turned away and walked down the dock towards the terminal.

Olivia sank down onto the bench. She shifted and pulled her skirt down to keep her thighs from getting scalded on the hot metal.

"He never said he was sorry. He never said he loved me." Olivia sighed. "I feel so stupid that I didn't see who he was before."

Hayley put her arm around Olivia's shoulders. "You weren't stupid. You trusted him."

Passengers heading home filled the enclosed walkway coming off of the ship. Crew, heading out to run errands before they had to be back on the ship for the next cruise, streamed off the crew gangway and across the dock towards the terminal.

Olivia rested her head on Hayley's shoulder.

She jolted upright.

"We just lost half of our show. What are we going to do?"

"We'll figure it out. He can't get Chico, that's all that matters. Anything else we will figure out."

Olivia's knee bounced up and down. "I can't believe he was going to take my parrot. He didn't even want Chico. He said that it would be too complicated to travel with a bird. I had to beg him to let me adopt him."

Hayley squeezed Olivia's hand. "You handled yourself really well with him."

Olivia slouched down on the bench and rubbed her face with her hands. "I need to go talk to Tristan and see if he can get a new act by the end of the cruise. We can do the show this week. Then I'll have to give Peter all of 'his' magic equipment. There's no way I could do a forty-five minute show with what will be left."

Hayley rubbed Olivia's back. "Is that what you want to do?"

"No!" Olivia jerked upright. "I don't know. I can't do the show with half of the illusions. It'll be a disaster."

"No, it won't. If you want to do the show, we'll figure it out. We'll do more stuff with Chico. Gail said she loved his part of the show and she'd love to see more of it. If the entertainment director says to add more of your parrot, you should totally add more of your parrot."

Olivia sat up. "You're right. She said that. But, we can't train him to do 20 minutes' worth of new tricks in one week."

"No, but we can go through what we have and see what we can do. If you want to stay on the ship, I know we can make it work."

The ship gleamed as the sun peaked through the clouds and hit its freshly painted side.

Visit WendyNeugentBooks.com

Wendy Neugent spent close to a decade as part of an award-winning magic act performing on cruise ships all over the world. She traveled from Alaska to Venezuela, Bermuda to Tahiti, and many exotic ports of call in between.

She now lives in Virginia with her husband, youngest son, and her Cornish Rex cat, Apurrham Lincoln.

Visit Wendy's website to see pictures from her cruise ship days and find information on new releases.

https://WendyNeugent.com/

Also By Wendy

Visit https://wendyneugent.com/books-in-order/ to see all of my books in order.

Get Gotcha! The prequel story of Chico's adoption for free Here: https://wendyneugent.com/free-book

Here is a little bit about Gotcha!

When Olivia walked into the pet store to buy dog food for her mother's chihuahua, she wasn't looking to adopt a pet.

After all, traveling the world as an entertainer on a cruise ship isn't exactly pet friendly.

But she desperately wants to save the bird from the nasty pet shop owner.

Not only is the pet shop owner mean to the little parrot, but Olivia suspects that he is up to no good.

Can she save the parrot and take down the pet store owner, or will the pet shop owner take Olivia out?

Get this mystery ebook for free and find out!

https://wendyneugent.com/free-book

Made in United States
Orlando, FL
31 August 2024